CAROLYN KEENE

NANCY DREW

GIRL DETECTIVE®

Serial Sabotage

#43

Aladdin Paperbacks
New York   London   Toronto   Sydney

❦ ALADDIN
An imprint of Simon & Schuster Children's Publishing Division
1230 Avenue of the Americas, New York, NY 10020
First Aladdin paperback edition October 2010
Text copyright © 2010 by Simon & Schuster
All rights reserved, including the right of reproduction in whole or in part in any form.
ALADDIN is a trademark of Simon & Schuster, Inc., and related logo is a registered trademark of Simon & Schuster, Inc.
NANCY DREW, NANCY DREW: GIRL DETECTIVE, and related logo are registered trademarks of Simon & Schuster, Inc.
For information about special discounts for bulk purchases, please contact Simon & Schuster Special Sales at 1-866-506-1949 or business@simonandschuster.com.
The Simon & Schuster Speakers Bureau can bring authors to your live event. For more information or to book an event contact the Simon & Schuster Speakers Bureau at 1-866-248-3049 or visit our website at www.simonspeakers.com.
Designed by Sammy Yuen Jr.
The text of this book was set in Bembo.
Manufactured in the United States of America
0910 OFF
10 9 8 7 6 5 4 3 2 1
Library of Congress Control Number 2010923695
ISBN 978-1-4169-9070-3
ISBN 978-1-4424-0960-6 (eBook)

Table of Contents

MISSING CASH BOX

"**F**ancy Nancy," Mrs. Gruen said, knocking on my bedroom door. "It's time to get up, dear. If it was left up to you, you would just sleep until noon and miss the parade completely. Now get up."

I opened my eyes slowly but didn't want to get up. The events of the previous day with the burn blog had completely exhausted me. Even though the burn blog mystery had been solved and Heather Harris busted for running the website, the threatening blue notes were still being written, and I had no idea who was behind them. Which was why I didn't want to get out of bed, but Mrs. Gruen, our housekeeper, kept knocking on my bedroom door until I could no longer go back to sleep.

"Fancy Nancy," she said again. "Are you awake, sweetie?"

"I'm awake," I said. "And why are you calling me that name?"

She didn't respond.

Classical music played quietly from the stereo in Dad's study. This particular composer I couldn't make out, as it sounded muffled through the floor, but I knew somewhere in the house Dad was conducting the orchestra. As far back as I could remember, Dad always loved classical music.

"Fancy Nancy, have you fallen back asleep? Don't make me come in there." I suddenly realized why Mrs. Gruen was calling me "Fancy Nancy." When Lexi Claremont asked me to solve the case of the mystery blogger, I'd had to go undercover to fit in with her clique—which meant dressing in stylish, expensive clothes that were hardly my usual style. Instead of comfortable jeans and T-shirts, I'd been wearing outfits Bess had helped me pick out, like the cashmere sweater and plaid mini I'd had on the day before yesterday. Well, as long as Mrs. Gruen didn't call me that in front of my friends, Bess and George, it was okay, but I also hoped she hadn't told Dad about it.

"You are going to miss the parade if you stay in bed any longer." Mrs. Gruen was a very kind and loving woman, taking care of both Dad and me, and so sweet. Who else would gently nudge me from my deep sleep and make sure that I made it to the River Heights Festival on time? She knew that if I was even ten minutes late, my good friend George would never let me hear the end of it.

I sat up in bed and was stretching my arms over my head when I smelled something amazing and delicious wafting up from the kitchen. I jumped out of bed and threw open the door. Mrs. Gruen stood in the hallway, a heavyset woman with her hair pulled back in a ponytail, her apron tied around her waist, arms folded over her chest.

"Is that what I think it is?" I asked.

"That depends on what you think it is," she said.

I took my time, breathing in slowly, savoring every second of air. "That smells like Mr. Andrews's banana bread."

Mrs. Gruen smiled. "I picked it up special just for you this morning."

I threw my arms around her neck and gave her the biggest hug I could muster this early in the morning. "Thank you. Thank you. Thank you so much."

"I know how much you like it, and he only makes it once a week, so in a sense I was forced to buy some. It's like I didn't even have a choice, really." She winked at me before walking downstairs to the kitchen.

Joshua Andrews owned the local River Heights Bakery. He made the most delicious foods throughout the week and served pretty good coffee. Not quite as good as Club Coffee, but respectable. The one thing that Mr. Andrews did best of all, though, was banana bread. Once a week for as long as I could remember, Mr. Andrews would bake his famous batch of banana bread, and the line of people waiting to buy it would extend out the door and down the block. You had to get there early; otherwise the supply would run out.

I ran downstairs to the kitchen and found the banana bread on the counter, still warm, and with walnuts today. I served myself a thick slice. It tasted incredible.

Dad entered the kitchen with the newspaper under his arm and a cup of coffee in his hand. He kissed me on the forehead and smiled at the bread. "Hannah got that special for us today." He was dressed for the office: suit pants, white button-down shirt, and an untied tie draped around his neck. His shirt and tie were both clean, without any stains, but the day was still early.

"I know," I said almost incoherently, as I chewed on an enormous mouthful of bread. "It's *soooooo* good."

Dad smiled, but his smile dropped off his face when he looked at his hands. They were covered in black ink. "I swear," he said. "The *River Heights Bugle* uses the worst ink. It comes right off on your fingers." He walked to the sink and scrubbed his hands under warm water and with a lot of soap. He finally sat down at the kitchen table and unfolded his paper as the orchestra played louder—a crescendo, as Dad once taught me. He extended his index fingers and began cueing invisible stringed instruments and horn sections and kettledrums. The ink on his fingers was fainter, but not completely gone.

Mrs. Gruen walked behind him and shook her head, laughing. "Carson, you do love your classical music. Maestro Drew should be your name."

Dad straightened his tie around his neck and began to tie it into a knot. "This is called a Windsor knot," he said, showing Mrs. Gruen and me. "All the famous conductors wear Windsor knots."

We both laughed at him, mocking his orchestral conducting by waving our index fingers through the air.

"Thank you again for getting this bread. It's my absolute favorite," I said.

"You know, Fancy Nancy," Mrs. Gruen finally said, "Joshua Andrews was acting pretty strange today about his bread."

"Really?" Dad said, adjusting his knot tight to his neck. "How so?"

"Well, I was the first one in line this morning, before he opened, and I overheard him on the phone inside. He was talking to Mark Steele."

"He's the head of the River Heights Carnival committee this year, isn't he, Nancy?" Dad asked.

"Yeah, but why would Mr. Steele be speaking with Mr. Andrews?" I asked.

"Like I said, it was early, and I was the first one in line outside waiting for the store to open, so I could hear Joshua loud and clear. And, boy oh boy, was he furious. Apparently, Mark Steele refused to let Joshua rent a table at the carnival to sell his banana bread."

"How strange," I said.

"Indeed," said Dad.

"The last thing I heard Joshua say was that he wasn't going to let Mark Steele bully him around anymore."

"Huh, I wonder why." I finished my banana walnut bread, got up from the table, and kissed Dad good-bye, before returning to my room to get ready for the carnival.

As I got dressed, I remembered all the advice Bess Marvin, one of my best friends and the girliest of girls I know, had given me about how to dress for the fro-yo stand, so that I wouldn't stand out from the other girls. It was part of my job to infiltrate their preppy clique and dress like them, but now that the mystery was solved, I wasn't sure if I even had to return to the fro-yo stand. I actually hadn't planned on returning, until Dad brought it to my attention that I had already committed to volunteering and that it would be bad form for me to cancel on them last minute. He was right, but he didn't know these girls. And it wasn't like I could just show up as me. I had to continue to fit in if I wanted to get through the day with my sanity intact.

I looked at myself in the mirror. Ugh, somewhere Bess was squealing again. Gray and blue mini. White polo shirt with a blue horse. Sunny yellow summer sweater draped over my shoulders, like Dad's tie. And cute, white strappy kitten heels. Ugh, I hated these kitten heels. What self-respecting detective runs around a carnival solving crimes in kitten heels? My feet still ached from wearing them all yesterday.

My gasoline-electric hybrid car that Dad had bought me for my birthday eased into an open spot in the high school parking lot. Across the way, I could see the ticket booth where Ned was supposed to be volunteering, but I couldn't see if anyone was inside yet. I was readjusting my sweater over my shoulders when a fist pounded down on the glass of my driver's side window.

"Nice outfit, Fancy Nancy. You ready to make fro-yos all day?" George said, still pounding her fist on my car.

My heart raced into my throat, and after a few seconds to collect myself I realized she had called me Fancy Nancy. I opened my door. "What did you just call me?"

"Nancy," she said.

"And?" I asked.

"Fancy in front of it. I called you Fancy Nancy. It was Mrs. Gruen. I called your house looking for you because you were, obviously, late and she said, 'Little Miss Fancy Nancy has already left for the carnival and will be there soon.'"

I rubbed my head. "Do not call me that. And do not let anyone find out about it. Okay?"

"Sure thing," George said, rummaging through her backpack.

"What do you have there?" I asked.

"I couldn't wait to show this to you. Check it out." She pulled a box from her bag and placed it in my hands. "It's my new high-tech NASA-developed Element Disintegration Chemistry Set. It was developed for space walks so astronauts could collect data from the moon rocks and stuff, but now it's used by crime scene investigators to analyze evidence."

Georgia "George" Fayne, George being her self-chosen nickname, of course, always made me smile, even if her nickname was way cooler than "Fancy Nancy." She was into her own things and didn't care what anyone else thought. She loved being a technology geek and a whiz at electronics. Her favorite hobby was to buy old, broken-down computers and rebuild them from scrap parts. She had five working laptops that I knew of and probably a few more that didn't work, waiting to be resurrected. This new über-science chemistry set was no different from the other hip-techno-supersleuth gadgets she spent her money on. But I had a feeling it would come in handy sooner than expected.

"George Fayne, where do you find out about these bizarre toys?"

"The Internet, naturally. And from my spy magazines. And my encyclopedias. And I read a lot of nonfiction about groundbreaking technology."

"Of course you do."

"Don't you read about plaid minis and summer sweaters?" she said, teasing me.

"Quiet," I said, locking my car behind me. "This outfit is in the name of fro-yo stands everywhere."

We walked across the parking lot together and could see that a long, somewhat unruly line had formed rather quickly at the carnival ticket booth. The line was ten people deep—each person grumbling and muttering under their breath. George and I bypassed the angry line and cut directly to the side door. We knocked several times, but without any answer. I was beginning to think that maybe everyone was so upset because no one was stationed at the booth collecting money for their tickets, but just then the door swung open from all my knocking.

It was Ned. He didn't realize George and I stood behind the door. He was clearly distraught. The booth looked like it had been hit by a tornado. Flipped and emptied boxes. Overturned chairs. Twisted blinds. Trash littered the floor.

"Ned," I said, stepping into the booth. "What's going on here?"

Ned turned, startled at first, but then threw his arms around me in a hug.

George looked at me, scared and confused, which was exactly how I felt, as this was not at all like Ned.

"Nancy. Nancy. I tried calling you. I am so glad you are here. I am in really big trouble. Super huge trouble." He was pacing now, his hand wiping sweat from his forehead and under his eyes. "I mean, people say that all the time, that they are in serious trouble, but I really mean it. Oh wow. Oh boy. I need to sit down. I don't feel good."

George turned one of the chairs upright and placed it under him. "Sit down," she told him. "We're here, Ned. How can we help?"

"Tell us what happened," I said. "Start from the beginning."

"I came in this morning and opened up the ticket booth, right?"

"Okay," I said.

"It was eight a.m., and the ticket booth wasn't supposed to open for another hour. People kept calling and stopping by, asking me questions, and asking me for favors. I was tired and just wanted to rest a bit and be left alone before I opened the booth, so I thought it wouldn't hurt if I just closed my eyes for a bit, you know. So I closed the door and rested. I didn't sleep, obviously. But just rested."

"Ned," I said. "What happened?"

"Well, I closed my eyes, and it was only for a few minutes, I swear, because I was going to open the blinds and windows and get the tickets ready to sell, but when I woke up . . ."

"When you woke up?" George asked.

"When I woke up, the cash box . . . the cash box was gone."

George and I looked at each other. Secretly and separately, I'm sure, we had both been hoping for a more relaxed day at the carnival, but here it was nine thirty in the morning and an angry mob of people milled outside the ticket booth, wanting to get into the carnival, but they couldn't because another crime had been committed. Another case had presented itself. Another question needed an answer.

"Have you told Mr. Steele yet? I asked.

"Not yet. It all just happened so fast. I thought I would be able to find it."

"Let's all three look around the booth before we sound the alarms and get people involved," I said. "Sometimes it's a simple solution to a seemingly scary situation."

"Good idea, Fancy Nancy," he said.

I shot him a look of disdain. "Mrs. Gruen?" I asked him.

"George, actually. She told me that you had a new nickname," he said.

George shrugged. "Now is not the time to be mad at me about your name. We have a cash box to find," she said.

All three of us began to clean the booth as a means to undo everything Ned had done and search for the missing cash box. We flipped chairs upright and untwisted the blinds and put the trash back into the trash can and packed miscellaneous items like T-shirts and tickets back into boxes. Before long, the booth was put back together, everything in its appropriate place, and we hadn't yet found the cash box.

"Oh boy," Ned said, sitting down. "Oh man. I am in very big trouble." He held his head in his hands.

"George, can you please go find Mr. Steele and ask him to come here? Ned, you need to stay calm and think about the last thing that you remember," I said.

But just as I said that, the door to the booth swung open and Mark Steele stormed inside. A short man, balding, his clothes baggy and oversized from the weight he'd lost recently—oh, and very angry.

"Nickerson, do you know what I just found outside in the trash can?"

"No, sir," Ned said, standing now.

I looked at George and whispered, "Looks like Mr. Steele is on the warpath."

"I found the cash box," said Mr. Steele.

"You did," Ned said, excited and somewhat relieved.

"Don't sound so happy, Nickerson," Mr. Steele said.

"Why is that, sir?" Ned asked.

Mr. Steele opened the metal box, flipped it upside down, and shook it, but nothing fell or floated out of it. It was empty. He tossed the empty cash box into Ned's lap.

"It's empty?" asked Ned, lifting it, shaking it,

running his fingers inside, hoping to find the money tucked away or stuck inside somewhere.

"Yes," Mr. Steele said. "And you're the last person in possession of it, so that begs the question: Ned Nickerson, why did you steal the River Heights Carnival money?"

FOUR SUSPECTS

"I'm afraid I am going to have to ask you to leave," Mr. Steele said, snapping his fingers at George and me, pointing at the door.

We slid along the wall of the ticket booth, careful to stay out of angry Mr. Steele's way, and stepped back outside. Mr. Steele slammed the door shut, but we could still hear his tirade inside as Ned tried to have a conversation. Ned sounded nervous and scared, I thought, because he felt bad about falling asleep, but something told me that there was more to this story. Someone was trying to frame him for the missing money, and I wasn't about to let that happen. I pressed my ear to the door to listen.

"Explain to me what happened, Ned. Where did the money go?" asked Mr. Steele. "It has been an hour and a half since I saw you last. How could this have happened?"

"Well, sir, I arrived at the ticket booth this morning, unlocked the door, and everything was in place. I counted out the cash box money and it was all there: three hundred and fifty dollars," Ned said.

"Ned, you understand that I have no choice but to involve the police? The carnival money is missing, and you cannot seem to shed any light on what happened here this morning," Mr. Steele said.

"Mr. Steele, I unlocked the ticket booth and turned on all the lights. The money was here. And I began answering phone calls. People kept calling with questions."

"What questions?" he asked.

"Like what time the parade began and what time the carnival opened."

"And no one else was in here with you?" Mr. Steele asked.

George grabbed my arm. "Nancy, should we go in there and help Ned?"

"No," I said. "We should stay out here and listen. The less Mr. Steele thinks we know, the more we'll be able to help Ned."

Ned continued, "A few people stopped by, but

there is no way they could have gotten to the cash box."

"Who?" Mr. Steele asked, his angry voice getting angrier, if that was even possible. "I would love to know who stopped by."

"Well, Deirdre Shannon stopped by," Ned said.

"For what? What could she possibly have needed?"

I looked at George and whispered, "Deirdre. We have our first suspect."

"Second suspect," George said. "Mr. Steele thinks Ned took the money. He's the first suspect."

As much as I hated to think about it, she was right. Ned was Suspect Number One.

Deirdre was Suspect Number Two.

Deirdre Shannon was a longtime acquaintance and former classmate of mine. Her father was a wealthy attorney, and she was always wearing the nicest clothes, so she would have no need for the carnival money. I couldn't imagine that she'd stolen it, but I also couldn't exclude her from the growing list of suspects. She was here before I arrived and therefore had to be considered as the possible thief. Not to mention the fact that she'd had a major crush on Ned for as long as I could remember. Maybe stopping by early in the morning was her way of flirting with him, but stealing the cash box money? It was too early to tell.

"What was Deirdre Shannon, the fro-yo stand girl, doing at the ticket booth?" Mr. Steele asked.

"She was carrying a few heavy boxes of cups and cones and ingredients for fro-yo, sir, and needed help getting them to her stand," he said. "But I told her that I couldn't help. I told her that I couldn't leave the ticket booth unattended. Because of the money."

"A lot of good that did you, kid. Who else stopped by?" asked Mr. Steele.

"Deirdre's boyfriend, Josh, that scruffy-looking kid who's always hanging around the fro-yo stand, he stopped by not too long after Deirdre," Ned said.

Bingo. Suspect Number Three.

If Deirdre had a crush on Ned, my all-American, clean-cut boyfriend, then it made sense that her real-life boyfriend was the exact opposite. Josh fit more into a "bad boy" mold, the troublemaker category. He was tall and scruffy, with shaggy dark hair, a lanky build, and three-day-old stubble covering his chin and jawline. Josh wore loose, vintage-looking jeans with a studded belt and a tight-fitting white T-shirt. He'd worn the same thing for the past two days, and I was sure he would be wearing the same thing again today.

"Ned, you're not instilling the greatest confidence here. What did he want?" Mr. Steele asked.

"He just asked to borrow some paper and a pen. I didn't ask what for, but he seemed really nervous and upset, so I just gave it to them. But neither Deirdre nor Josh stepped foot into the ticket booth. Not one foot, sir. I made sure they stayed right outside."

"Did you turn your back on them at all?" asked Mr. Steele.

"Yes, sir, but it was only for a few seconds at most."

"Sometimes, Ned, all it takes is a couple of seconds."

I wondered how many times in his life that grumpy old Mark Steele had said that sentence: *Sometimes all it takes is a couple of seconds.*

"I'm sorry, Mr. Steele. I really am, but the only other person who I saw this morning was Mara Stanfield. She stopped by, but just to make sure there was a volunteer working the ticket booth."

Mara Stanfield, Suspect Number Four.

"That's right, Ned. You are a volunteer. You offered to work this morning. We are not paying you to work, are we?"

"No, sir."

"Well, then. As far as I can see, you are my number one suspect. You had access to the cash box and you have motive."

"What motive?" he asked. "I would never steal money."

"Son, your motive is not being paid. I'm sorry, but I am calling Chief McGinnis. I need to report this as a theft. To be honest, I'm not entirely convinced that you're telling me the truth."

"Oh, no. Nancy, what do we do?" George looked shocked and covered her mouth with her hand. "Ned is going to get arrested."

As much as Mr. Steele thought he had this crime solved, his understanding of motive was wildly wrong. He should stick to teaching high schoolers and leave the mysteries to professionals. Chief McGinnis would understand that Ned didn't take the money. I mean, where would he have stashed it? And that was all hinging on the fact that Ned had time to get away from the ticket booth. Between answering all the phone call questions and dealing with Deirdre, Josh, and Mara, when would he have taken the money? Or taken a real nap, for that matter?

Also, if Ned volunteered to work at the ticket booth, then he understood that he wouldn't get paid. That wasn't a motive. That was a fact. Now, if Ned had been forced to work at the ticket booth as some kind of punishment, then Mr. Steele would have a motive to pin to Ned.

This was all driving me crazy. I just want to burst

into the ticket booth the same way Mr. Steele had done earlier and argue my case, but I knew better. If I was to help Ned, I needed to be subtle and almost invisible.

"Nancy, what do you want to do?" George asked.

"We have our suspects, George. But we need to find Bess to help us investigate. Have you heard from her at all?" I asked.

"Bess told me that she was arriving here early to inspect the float for the parade. But I haven't seen her yet," said George.

The door to the ticket booth swung open, and Mark Steele stepped out. Ned followed quickly behind and ran to me with a worried look in his eyes. Mr. Steele stood by the street, checking his watch and looking over his shoulder occasionally. He looked like he was about to rocket into outer space, fueled by anger. Ned just looked scared. I knew that he hadn't taken the money, and it was now up to me to solve the mystery.

"Nancy, I didn't do it. You have to believe me," Ned said.

"I do believe you. Don't worry. I just need some time to investigate and snoop around. I'm sure I'll uncover who took the cash box money."

A River Heights Police Department car pulled up to the curb in front of the ticket booth, and Chief McGinnis got out. He was a very tall man; over six feet, with bushy dark eyebrows and a large gut that hung over his police belt. I knew Chief McGinnis better than he knew me. Over the years, he had taken credit for many of the mysteries I had solved myself, but being a high school kid and not an official police officer, I was okay with that. My biggest problem with Chief McGinnis was the way he talked about a crime. He sounded so corny sometimes, like he was some kind of private investigator from an old black-and-white detective movie.

"Howdy," Chief McGinnis said to Mr. Steele.

Gosh, he was cheesy. Who said the "howdy" anymore?

"Hey, Chief," Mr. Steele said. "I got a really easy case here. I need you to arrest Ned Nickerson."

Chief McGinnis laughed and placed his hand on his hip.

"What's so funny?" said Mr. Steele.

"If I had a dollar every time someone asked me to arrest a person, I could retire to Florida in peace and leave this entire police racket behind," he said.

"I mean it, Chief. I'm serious. Please arrest Ned Nickerson."

"I know you're serious, Mark."

"Ned Nickerson stole the ticket booth money."

"Okay, well, give me the facts," Chief said. "Just the facts."

Just the facts? Oh, jeez! This was going to be a long day.

Mark Steele put his arm around Chief McGinnis and spoke to him quietly. Both men looked up at Ned. Mr. Steele nodded accusingly in Ned's direction as they walked out into the parking lot for privacy.

Just then Bess bounced across the parking lot with her shoulder-length blond hair and dimples, waving her arms in the air, running past the men. She sprinted toward us as we stood outside the ticket booth. It was great to see her, but George was always the one more likely to run across a parking lot, not Bess. George always had the new gadgets and gizmos that she couldn't wait to show people. Bess was always extra careful, careful not to fall, not to mess up her new coat of nail polish, careful not to embarrass herself. Except for today. Bess definitely had something important to tell us.

The mob of people waiting to enter the carnival had gotten smaller since several other volunteers had arrived. They had obtained more money for the ticket booth and were making change for people to purchase tickets to gain entrance. Mr. Steele didn't want to draw attention to the issue of the missing money and tried very hard to keep even Chief McGinnis's presence from causing a stir.

"Fancy Nancy," Bess said, finally stopping and

catching her breath. She bent over, resting her hands on her knees.

"Seriously, what is with everyone calling me Fancy Nancy today?"

Bess looked at George, and they both smirked.

"Nancy, I saw Chief McGinnis," Bess said. "What's happening?"

"They think Ned stole the cash box money," George explained.

Bess stood up straight and caught her breath. She put her hand on my shoulder and said, "Follow me." She walked in front of us as she approached the Chief and Mr. Steele, stopping a few feet away from them. They didn't acknowledge all of us standing there, so Bess cleared her throat so incredibly loudly that George and I started laughing. Ned didn't think it was funny, but then again, he was being accused of stealing, so he didn't have much of a sense of humor about the situation.

"What is it?" Mr. Steele asked, scowling. He obviously didn't think it was funny either.

"Ned didn't steal your money," said Bess. "He's innocent."

"If I had a dollar for every time a random stranger told me someone was innocent, I could buy a boat down in Florida and sail all around the world," said Chief McGinnis.

"He didn't steal it," Bess insisted. "I was the first person here this morning. Mara Stanfield asked me to be here in case the carpenters delivered the Daughter of River Heights float early."

"Why you?" Mr. Steele asked.

"Because I helped sketch the design and directed the carpenter crew to make certain alterations, and Mara wanted me here to inspect the float first thing."

"Well, where is it?" said Mr. Steele, his hands on his hips. "The float? I don't see it."

"It hasn't come yet," Bess said, getting a little annoyed. "But please listen. Ned arrived and never left the booth. Not once. If he never left the booth, then where did he stash the money? All you have to do is check his pockets and belongings."

Chief McGinnis rubbed his forehead. "Not that I don't believe you, but as a test, who else did you see this morning? Was there anyone else hanging around?" he asked Bess, testing her, I thought. Seeing if her story matched what Ned had claimed happened.

Without any hesitation, Bess replied, "Deirdre Shannon, her boyfriend Josh, and Mara Stanfield. In that order, too. They each stopped by separately, but Ned never once left the booth. He didn't even let them *in* the booth."

Chief and Mr. Steele approached Ned and asked

him to step back inside the ticket booth. I ran to the door and pressed my ear to it again. I was so nervous that the chief wouldn't do a thorough job and would simply put the blame on Ned. He was a volunteer, after all. Why would he have taken the money? Inside, they asked Ned to open his book bag and empty his pockets. Moments later, the door swung open and Ned came running out, a giant smile on his face.

"They don't think I stole the money anymore," he said.

I turned to Bess and George, both equally as excited that Ned was off the hook, but a little scared-looking, like they knew I was about to enlist their help in solving another crime.

"We have three suspects now, gang. Deirdre, who has always had a crush on Ned. Josh, who could be jealous of Deirdre's crush on Ned. And Mara, who doesn't really seem to have a motive at all," I said.

"What do you want us to do, Nancy?" George asked.

"George, I want you to shadow Josh. Follow his every move. See if he starts spending a lot of money. Anyone who steals three hundred and fifty dollars is either going to spend it right away or try and hide it until they think no one is watching before they retrieve it. And Bess," I said.

"You want me to keep an eye on Mara," she said before I even had a chance.

"Something weird is going on here, and I think she might know something."

"What are you going to do, Nancy?" Ned asked.

"I have to go to work. Don't you see how I'm all dressed up?"

"Fancy Nancy," George, Bess, and Ned all said at the same time, before erupting into laughter.

"Okay, which one of you started this name?"

They all either looked at their shoes or over my shoulder, like they saw someone they might know. Regardless, no one answered my question. I wasn't totally surprised by their silence.

"Well, I'm going to work and see what I can find out from Deirdre. I'm late for the fro-yo stand," I said, looking at my watch. "Actually, *really* late for the fro-yo stand."

ANOTHER BLUE NOTE

" **Y**ou couldn't be any later if you tried," Deirdre Shannon said, snapping a bubble with her gum. "We can run this fro-yo stand without you, you know? Your presence is not necessary."

All four girls stood behind the stand, not particularly happy to see me—Heather, Lexi, Aly, and Deirdre.

Heather Harris was still angry about getting busted yesterday for writing the hatethesegirls.com website and seemed equally sheepish around the other girls. She didn't look me in the eyes and kept distancing herself from me. Frankly, I was surprised she'd shown up at all. If I were her, I'm not sure I would be able to come back to the fro-yo stand.

Lexi Claremont, I thought, was annoyed that I'd shown up today, since the website mystery was already solved. She had only invited me to help out so that I could get closer to her friends to uncover the mystery blogger. I hadn't really wanted to come back, but Dad was right: I'd made the commitment to volunteer at the stand this weekend, and I should stick it out. I needed to be here anyway, to keep an eye on Deirdre Shannon. I couldn't believe that, after everything, she still had her sights set on Ned.

And then, of course, there was Aly Stanfield, whose mother was Mara Stanfield. I wondered if maybe she knew something.

This was going to be a peculiar day to navigate.

"Did you hear me?" said Deirdre.

"We don't need you here anymore," Lexi reiterated. "You did enough yesterday. Speaking of which," she added, turning to Heather, "I'm honestly surprised you had the nerve to show up today."

Heather shrugged and looked at her feet.

There were no customers this early in the morning, which only fueled the distrust and complicated relationships among all of us.

"If Heather didn't show up and I didn't show up and the fro-yo stand got hit by a long line later today, you would wish we were here to help out," I pointed out.

"I think we'd be okay," Aly said. "My mom wouldn't let the fro-yo stand suffer like that."

"Yeah, your tardiness is unacceptable," said Lexi.

All I wanted to do was walk away from this silly fro-yo stand right now, but I knew that I had an obligation to Ned and to the River Heights Carnival to find the missing money.

"If you must know why I was late," I said, "I was talking with Mr. Steele and Chief McGinnis. Someone stole the carnival ticket booth money, and my *boyfriend*, Ned Nickerson, was a suspect." I emphasized the word "boyfriend" for Deirdre's benefit.

The girls looked at one another, shocked, confused, maybe even a little nervous.

"Did they find the money?" Lexi asked.

"Not yet," I said.

"Does my mom know?" asked Aly.

"Not yet," I said.

"Does Chief McGinnis have any leads?" Heather asked.

"Three," I said.

Deirdre was the only girl who didn't ask a question. I walked behind the stand and stood next to her.

"I arrived this morning and Mr. Steele called the chief to arrest Ned for stealing the money from the cash box. Thankfully, there was an eyewitness who exonerated Ned, so they let him off the hook, but the thief is still out there somewhere." I pointed to the passing crowds of people, walking by wearing sunglasses and applying sunscreen, standing in line for big pretzels or waiting to ride the Ferris wheel. "It could be anyone, but it's most likely one of three leads."

"Who are the three leads?" Heather asked.

"Don't worry, Heather," I said. "You're not one of them."

"That's really good news, Fancy Nancy," Heather said.

All the girls broke out into hearty fits of laughter. This was getting truly ridiculous. The name seemed to be spreading faster than a fire, and there was no end in sight. Someone knew that the name would really bother me, and they were making it their mission to annoy me into insanity!

Heather released a sigh of relief, which I knew she would. But I also refused to let the girls find out that easily who I was considering as the cash box thief. I still wasn't sure there was any connection between the thief and the person leaving the notes. I just didn't have enough information yet.

I walked to the cash box of the fro-yo stand and opened the lid slowly, letting the girls watch me, probably wondering what I was doing. All the money seemed to still be there.

"Well, that's a good sign," I said. "Glad to see *we* still have all of *our* money."

Deirdre finally snapped and stormed toward me.

"You really think I did it? You really think I would steal the cash box money? Do I need to call my father? You do realize he is the most powerful defense attorney in River Heights. Your father certainly knows that well," Deirdre said. Our fathers often found themselves facing each other in court on either side of the law. "I have absolutely zero motive to steal the stupid money. Besides, Heather seems the more obvious suspect. She got busted yesterday for that stupid website. Seems to me like she would want to get back at everyone. Maybe even try and frame me."

"It's wasn't me," Heather said. "I didn't do it."

"You did start hatethesegirls.com," said Lexi.

"Well, you stole my boyfriend," Heather shot back.

"Deirdre, I never said that any of you were suspects," I said. "I never even mentioned *you* as a suspect. But now that you mention it, what were you doing at the ticket booth this morning?"

"I am a pleasant person, Nancy. I say good morning to people. I had just arrived and was carrying a lot of materials for the fro-yo stand and happened to be passing the ticket booth," Deirdre said.

"And so you said hello to Ned, but you didn't ask him for help or talk to him at all, other than to say good morning?"

"Do you think I'm some kind of helpless girl who can't carry cups and cones and napkins for our stand? No, I didn't ask for his help. I said good morning to him and then asked him if he had seen Josh."

"Why?" I ask.

"Josh told me he would meet me at my car to help carry the fro-yo stand supplies, but he never showed up," said Deirdre. "So I carried them myself. I never asked Ned to help me. He offered. But I declined."

"According to Ned and Bess, Josh stopped by the ticket booth too. He was looking for a piece of paper and pen, apparently," I said. "You must have just passed each other."

Deirdre looked out into the crowds, like she was looking for an answer. I had seen that look a hundred times before. Confused. Bewildered. I'd started to think that maybe Deirdre and Josh were in on the heist together, but that vacant, lost look on Deirdre's face told me otherwise. She seemed genuinely confused about the Josh sighting.

"Did you talk to him? Did he say why he was there?" she asked. "Or why he didn't meet me at my car?"

"Not yet, but that is definitely on my list of things to do today," I said as our first customer approached the fro-yo stand. "Just like serving fro-yo is on my list of things to do." I turned to the customer and smiled. "Hi, how are you? Welcome to our fro-yo stand. What can I get for you today?"

The man smiled back and crossed his arms over his chest. It was my father, Carson Drew. "I heard about all the chaos and commotion this morning with Ned and the missing money. I ran over as soon as possible," he said.

"Can I offer you a special vanilla fro-yo in our commemorative River Heights cup?" I asked, letting my father continue to talk about the Ned situation while I remained out of it. If any of these girls were in on the theft, they would surely get nervous listening to him talk about it.

"Did everything sort itself out?" he asked. "Did they find the money?"

"Or you can have your fro-yo in one of our giant-sized waffle cones," I said. "Deirdre carried the cones all the way from her car."

"Nancy, why are you ignoring me? Is everything okay here? Did Mr. Steele recover the money?" he asked.

"Would you like any special daily toppings? Like coconut? Or pecans?" I asked, ignoring him. Just then I noticed Deirdre step back behind the other girls and disappear. The moment I thought Deirdre Shannon could be innocent and scratched off the suspects list, she snuck away. If she had stolen the money, I wondered where she'd hidden it and how she planned on spending it. Better still, why? All these questions kept begging for answers. I couldn't wait to meet up with Bess and George to find out how their suspects were faring.

"I didn't want to arouse their suspicions," I whispered. "They didn't find the money yet. Mr. Steele wanted Chief McGinnis to arrest Ned for the crime, but we were able to exonerate him. So right now, there are three leading suspects."

Dad uncrossed his arms and laughed. "You can get in a lot of trouble sometimes, Fancy Nancy," he said.

The other girls laughed when they heard this name. I was losing my sleuthlike edge over the girls. All my wit and posturing were gone now that they had heard my father call me Fancy Nancy.

"Dad, why is everyone calling me Fancy Nancy today?" I asked. "This is the true mystery. Not who stole the carnival ticket money, but rather who started calling me this silly and very embarrassing name."

Dad laughed again. "I have *no* idea," he said. "I thought we always called you Fancy Nancy."

"No," I said, rubbing my eyes, annoyed. "You have

never called me that. I think this all has to do with Mrs. Gruen somehow. She's putting you and Bess and George up to this."

"I think I will get a fro-yo, after all. Vanilla. In a regular cone, please."

I walked over to the machine and began to pour the frozen yogurt into an expert spiral. "Toppings?" I asked, but Dad shook his head no. I wrapped the base of the cone in a napkin and handed it to him. It didn't take long for Mr. Carson Drew, Esquire, to spill a giant glob of fro-yo on his tie.

"Oh jeez," Dad said. "I'm always spilling on my ties." He rubbed at the stain with his fingers. "Fancy Nancy, could you hand me another napkin, please?"

Although part of me wanted to let him suffer the humiliation of another stain on his tie for calling me that name again, I had to help him. I looked back to where the napkins had been placed before on the table and could no longer find them.

"Lexi, Aly, Heather, any of you seen the napkins?" I asked.

Lexi and Aly pretended not to hear me as Heather helped me to look. Unfortunately, we couldn't find them. Just as I was about to walk across the way to the hot dog stand and borrow a stack of their napkins, I saw it—another blue note.

Heather stood back from it like it was a live snake

about to bite her. Aly and Lexi both dropped their jaws in shock, but neither wanted to pick it up. Finally, I did.

"What you got there?" Dad asked.

"Another blue note," I said.

"Another bad note?" Heather asked.

I looked at the words scribbled across the blue paper. "It's not nice."

At the hot dog stand, I heard gasps and exclamations. One by one, each of the stands around us found similar blue notes with, I assumed, similar threats written on them. We all had received a warning. Someone was not going to stop until the River Heights Carnival was shut down.

"Well," Lexi said, "what does the note say?"

I read the note out loud.

Everyone felt the same shiver crawl up their spine.

FOOD COURT QUESTIONS

G eorge and I sat in the food court section of the carnival as I finished retelling the blue note story to her.

"Well, what does the note say?" George said, irritated that I'd ended my fro-yo story on such an enormous cliffhanger. "Nancy, you really can't end a story like that. Completely unresolved. You are the worst storyteller. EVER!"

I took out the blue note from my purse and handed it to her. It read:

THIS IS ANOTHER WARNING.
LEAVE THE CARNIVAL.

NOW.
OR ELSE.

"And we weren't the only stand that got this note. A whole bunch of us did," I said. "They each said the same thing."

"This has gotten very serious," said George.

"We really don't have much time to find out who's behind the stolen money. I'm guessing they're also behind the blue notes."

People walked about, eating all the different kinds of carnival food available. I glanced around, looking for a table where Joshua Andrews and his River Heights Bakery were selling his food, but didn't see him. In fact, I saw every kind of food except his. I wondered if Mrs. Gruen was on to something about him being mad at Mr. Steele for not letting him set up a table. Could the man responsible for the most delicious banana nut bread in all of River Heights also be responsible for stealing the carnival ticket money and the random blue notes? Not to mention all the earlier sabotage?

"Any leads on Deirdre Shannon?" George asked.

"Not really. She disappeared from the fro-yo stand after a while, but I did have a chance to confront her. Something tells me Deirdre isn't malicious enough to steal money from the carnival. She might not be my favorite person in the world, but I don't think she could do it. I think she's more afraid of being accused of the crimes."

"Your instincts are normally right," George said. "If you believe that to be true, then so do I."

"What about your suspect—Josh, Deirdre's boyfriend? Find out anything interesting on him?" I asked.

George laughed and pointed across several picnic tables.

Josh sat there, hunched over, shoveling food into his mouth. Laid out in front of him was one of every type of carnival food. Corn dog. Hot dog. Pink cotton candy. Oversize salted pretzel. Nachos with jalapeños and cheese. A caramel apple. A paper bag of popcorn. Funnel cake. Italian ice. And a bottle of water.

"My word," I said. "Look at all the food."

"I know," George said. "I think he must be going for a record or something. No one in their right mind would eat *every* single kind of food at a carnival, right?"

"Do you think he's spending the ticket money on food?" I asked.

"He's been sitting here the entire time. He takes a bite of this and a bite of that. It's like he's trying to win a bet or something," said George.

"So he hasn't been spending any money?" I asked.

"No. That's the weird thing. He isn't spending money on anything. People just keep bringing him food. It's like he's the official taste tester of the carnival. He hasn't spent one dime," George said.

Josh took another bite from the funnel cake and then a bite from his caramel apple, before washing it down with a gulp of water.

"Fancy Nancy, can I see the note again?" George said.

"If you tell me who is behind this 'Fancy Nancy' mystery, I will give you the note. Who started it?" I asked.

"I could never reveal my source." George laughed.

I handed her the note and watched Josh shovel more food into his mouth. George looked at the note close to her face, like she was an old lady who needed reading glasses. She turned the blue paper in her hand, holding it at the edges very gently. She held it out from her, looking at it from a distance, and then brought it close to her eyes again. She looked like she was playing the trombone.

"You know what?" she asked. "I just had the greatest idea." George looked over her shoulder toward the high school, before looking back to the note. It was clear that she had a thought in her head and she was turning it around, flipping it over, looking at it from all sides. And it was driving me crazy that she wouldn't spit it out!

"Well . . . what?" I asked. "You really can't leave a person on such a huge cliffhanger, George! You are the world's worst storyteller!"

"My new high-tech NASA–developed Element Disintegration Chemistry Set," she said.

"And why would that help?"

"Well, see this black smudge?" she asked, pointing to one of the corners of the paper. "My Element Disintegration Chemistry Set (EDCS for short) should be able to tell us what that smudge is and where it came from. Crime scene investigators use this all the time, apparently, to analyze prints and smudges. It helps them to eliminate suspects from their list."

"Really? George, that's fantastic! Do you think it will help us find out who is writing the notes?" I asked.

"I'm not sure about that, but it will tell us what these black smudges are at the corners, and that should help us narrow down the list," she said.

"And that would certainly be another clue in this big crazy puzzle of a mystery," I said. "George, you go do that now. I'll keep an eye on Josh." I couldn't stop watching Josh, eating all that food, as someone brought him a hamburger. I looked back at George, who was smiling. I had a feeling she was absolutely relieved to leave and not have to watch him eat any more food.

"Excellent idea!" she said, standing. She ran across the food court, disappearing into the side entrance of the high school.

Josh continued to chomp away at the food in front of him without a care in the world. Although my expertise and experience told me he probably had nothing to do with either the notes or the missing money, I still needed to know why he'd borrowed paper and a pen this morning. I needed to know why he'd asked Ned for those items. The only way to truth was with facts. As Chief McGinnis would say, I needed cold, hard facts. I needed the truth.

I walked over to his table and sat down across from him. He struggled to swallow a mouthful of food. I pushed his bottle of water over to him, which he accepted and gulped down. As he finished, he gasped for air.

"Thanks, Fancy Nancy," he said. "That last bite nearly killed me." He rubbed his stomach. "I am so stuffed."

There it was again! Who was going around telling people to call me Fancy Nancy? Someone was behind all this, but I needed to solve the missing money mystery first.

"This looks like a lot of food, Josh," I said. "Hungry much?"

"I'm friends with all the food stand owners. They like to use me as their guinea pig. You know, make sure their food is as good as last year." He took another sip of water. "It *is* all as good as last year. But I am so full."

"I don't see a fro-yo," I said. "Deirdre didn't bring you one?"

"No. She and I are kind of in an argument right now," he said. "She's mad at me for not meeting her at her car this morning, and I didn't like that she was hanging around Ned earlier. No offense to you, but she's always had a bit of a crush on him."

"Is that why you went to see him this morning?" I asked. "To confront him?"

"How did you know about that?"

"Word got around about the cash box getting stolen. Chief McGinnis questioned a lot of people about who could have stolen the money, and your name came up."

"Me?" He looked shocked, his eyes finally looking at me straight on. "I didn't do it. I really didn't. I like Ned. I just don't like that Deirdre likes Ned."

"I can't help the fact that you're a suspect," I said.

"I didn't steal the money."

"I believe you."

"Nancy, I swear to you on my driver's license that I didn't take that money."

"Driver's license?" I asked.

"It's my most valuable possession. I would never steal from anyone. Not money. Not anything. I swear to you. Who thinks I stole it?"

"No one. Yet. People just said that they saw you stop by the ticket booth this morning," I said. "So let me ask the obvious question: Did you stop by the ticket booth this morning to see Ned?"

"I did stop by, but I didn't steal any money."

"Then let me help you," I said. "Why did you go to the ticket booth? You can understand why people would be suspicious. You're not volunteering to help out. You're not working at the carnival. You're sitting here eating a ton of food. Apparently, not paying for it. You have to admit it looks awfully incriminating. There was no reason for you to be here that early."

Josh looked around, like people were still watching him. He rubbed his eyes, then his temples. He looked pale, and his skin began sweating. Clearly he was nervous about something, and he wasn't telling me anything new about why he borrowed paper. I began moving his food away from him, sliding it along the table. He closed his eyes, probably thankful I was removing it from his sight.

"Josh, why did you stop by the ticket booth this morning?" I asked again.

"You want the truth?" he asked. "I can't believe I'm going to actually tell someone about this."

"Please," I said. "Tell me."

"I asked Ned if I could borrow some paper."

"To write a note?" I asked.

"Yes," he said.

"And was it blue?"

"Yeah."

I couldn't believe it. Was Josh the one who had been writing the notes? It made sense, though. Every food stand had been given a threatening note, and he sat at the picnic table eating something from each of the stands. Maybe he was threatening all of them so he could get free food. Except the note we received at the fro-yo stand didn't say anything about receiving free food. And why would he ask Ned for paper to write notes, if he knew the notes could be traced back to him?

"I didn't take the money," he said. "All I did was ask Ned if I could borrow some paper and a pen."

"To write the food stand notes," I said. "I know. I really appreciate you coming forward with that information."

"No, wait a minute. I only wrote one note. And it wasn't to any of the food stands." He stopped rubbing his temple. "What are you talking about?"

"What are *you* talking about?" I asked. "Aren't you the one who's been threatening everyone?"

"No, I'm the one who—," he started. Then he began again in a whisper. "I am the one who got in a car accident with a parked car and left a note on their windshield."

"Excuse me? I asked, completely blindsided by his admission of guilt. Unfortunately, it was guilt for a random innocent crime.

"I drove my parents' car to the carnival this morning. I was on my way to meet Deirdre. I was supposed to arrive early, meet her at her car, and help her carry the fro-yo supplies to the stand. The only problem was . . . I was parking in the parking lot when I got distracted by a song on the radio. I slammed into the car parked next to me when I was backing up into the spot. I scratched the whole side of both cars, but since no one was around and no one witnessed it, I had a choice. I could either park somewhere else and act like it never happened or leave a note on the other car with an explanation of what happened and give them all my information."

"So you went to Ned at the ticket booth and asked to borrow a sheet of paper and a pen to write your note," I said.

"I did the responsible thing and am holding myself accountable for my actions, but I am not going to be blamed for the stolen money. I didn't do that."

"Like I said before, I believe you." I felt sorry for him, honestly. He did the right thing by leaving the note, the responsible thing, something my dad would have been very happy about. Although he wouldn't have been happy about the scratches on his car.

Josh stood and waved for me to stand too. He walked toward the parking lot.

"Where are we going?" I asked. "I said that I believe you."

"I want to show you the scratches and the note. My car is right there," Josh said, pointing.

We walked across the lot to a grove of trees, shading the cars from the midday sun. We reached the cars, and Josh pointed to the long zigzag scratches along the sides of both cars. Flapping in the quiet breeze, tucked under the windshield wiper of the other car, was another blue note. I pulled it out and unfolded it. It read:

Dear Madam or Sir:
I accidentally hit your car when parking my own car.
Below is my insurance and personal information.
I am very sorry.
Josh

I put the note back. He left the note to be responsible and was eating to distract himself from his fear. I felt sorry for him and began to tell him about a great mechanic that Dad and I used who was an expert at dents and scratches, but when I turned around, Josh ran past me, shouting, "See? Oh man, my parents are going to be so mad."

Josh was innocent. Another dead end.

As I walked back toward the carnival, I wondered how long it would be before something else went wrong. How long would it be before another note was found? How long would it be before another carnival ride was sabotaged? How much more money would be stolen? I felt stuck in this mystery, with every solid lead falling apart. I hoped George could work her magic and figure out what those smudges were, and I hoped Bess was having better luck with her suspect.

5

DAUGHTERS OF RIVER HEIGHTS FLOAT ARRIVES

Bess stood by herself, leaning up against the ticket booth, looking at the new coat of polish on her nails. She looked bored as she waited for someone. She finally looked up at me as I crossed the parking lot on my way back from Josh's car.

"Fancy Nancy," she said. "I've been looking for you."

"Really?" I asked. "Are you ready to tell me who started this silly nickname business? I really would love to know."

"No, but I have some information about Mara Stanfield."

Just then Mara appeared from behind the ticket booth with her purse in her hand.

"Whoa, look at that purse," Bess said.

"What's wrong with it?"

"Nothing. It's beautiful. And not some knockoff, either."

"How do you know?" I asked.

"It's a Prada purse. See the logo clasp? Very expensive. Very hard to copy. That is an authentic, real-deal Prada purse. So beautiful."

I didn't really understand what Bess was talking about, but she seemed to know a thing or two about accessories like this, so I took her word for it.

When I finally looked up from the purse and at Mara, she had a scowl on her face that terrified me. If she were a cartoon character, steam would have shot out of her ears. Her eyes would have been bright red and her nostrils flaring. She stormed past us and toward a giant tractor-trailer pulling into the parking lot. Behind the tractor-trailer was the Daughter of River Heights float, the one that Bess had been put in charge of overseeing the alterations for. Mara stood with her hands on her hips, waiting for the driver to park and shut off its engine.

"I will not let this parade start late, and if it does, it will not be my fault. I swear I cannot handle this right now. There is too much to do," she said to herself.

Her foot tapped fast. She crossed her arms over her chest as she waited.

Finally the driver parked and hopped out of his cab with a signature pad for someone to sign on delivery of the float.

"You have some nerve showing up an hour late," Mara said to him.

"Sorry, ma'am," he said. "Someone from your organization gave me bad directions."

Bess immediately began playing with her hair, looking in the opposite direction, away from the driver and Mara. I thought for a minute that the float's late arrival might be another attempt at sabotaging the carnival and parade, but quickly realized it had to do with Bess.

I nudged her with my elbow and whispered, "Did you give him the directions?"

"*Nan-cy*," she whispered back. "Oh my gosh . . . shush . . . don't draw any attention to me. You are going to get me in some serious trouble. I thought they were good directions."

Mara continued, "I don't care what directions you were given or who exactly gave them to you, but you are late, and I want a price reduction on the alterations."

"I can't do that," he said. "You'll need to contact the home office and negotiate a rate change with them."

I leaned back over to Bess, who still was not acting normal, and filled her in on all the new information I had about the notes and Deirdre and Josh and the missing money. I showed her the fro-yo stand note and told her about Josh's car accident.

"We have more notes than we know what to do with," I said. "What is it with people and notes? It's like they actively hate text messages."

"Josh and Deirdre didn't do it?" Bess asked.

"The evidence doesn't support them as suspects anymore. They had access to the money, but their motives don't hold up. Their actions are certainly bizarre, and I still don't trust either of them wholly, but I feel like they told me the truth for the most part."

"I wouldn't want to be in Josh's position with the car accident, but I'm glad everyone is okay," said Bess. As we watched Mara argue with the driver, Bess kept hanging her head, ashamed that she'd given bad directions.

"And what about Mara?" I asked, nodding in her direction as she paced back and forth behind the driver, yelling into her cell phone, demanding a discount from the person on the phone.

"It wasn't Mara," she said. "She's been complaining about this float all day and how the money for it was in the cash box and was stolen too. She had to pay for it out of pocket, even though she's getting reimbursed by Mr. Steele later today. She's not losing money, but she was really mad about the cash box situation. The carnival is still paying for the float, so why would she steal the money to make herself pay out of pocket?"

"Good point," I said. "Seems like a lot of emotional anguish and stress to put yourself through just to steal a few hundred dollars."

Mr. Steele exited the school and approached the driver and Mara, which reminded me that George was somewhere inside, running her chemistry test for us. He walked quickly toward the pair, pulling out a wallet, counting out cash even quicker. Mara hung up the phone and argued some more with the driver, but they were too far away for us to hear exactly what was said. Eventually, Mr. Steele handed the driver a wad of cash and spoke to Mara quietly as the driver unloaded the float from the back of his trailer and into the parking lot.

"Did you see that?" I asked Bess. "She didn't have to pay after all. Mr. Steele did. Out of *his* own pocket."

Mara walked over to us, snapping her fingers. "Bess, I need you to hop up there," she said, pointing to the float. "Please check on our alterations, pronto. Before this hooligan leaves with his trailer." Then she leaned in closer and said, "Did you see Mr. Steele pay for everything right away?"

"I did," Bess said, appeasing her.

"This missing cash box ordeal has been a real nightmare for all of us today. I just hope the parade goes off without a hitch."

Bess smiled at Mara, before running across the parking lot to the float. She climbed the stairs of the boat-shaped vessel and walked around the deck. She checked the railing, pulling and pushing on it. She measured the throne and the platform and tested the sturdiness of the flagpole that rose up out of the center. Everything seemed to be sturdy and to her liking. She lifted a thumb in the air to Mara, who gave her a thumbs-up back. Then Bess looked at her hand and ran back across the parking lot to us. She was close to out of breath when she reached us. She lifted up her hand.

"Only thing is that the paint is still drying in certain areas." Her entire hand was covered in red paint.

Mara sighed and covered her eyes with her hands. "This is just another disaster."

"It's not that bad," Bess said. "We could get a hair dryer and hold it to the wet spots. Or it might even be dry by the time we start the parade."

A voice passing by interrupted us. It was Mr. Andrews, the baker.

"Your float is not a disaster," he said with eyes on Mr. Steele. "Not having a food stand, now *that* is a disaster." His hands were fists by his side, and they pumped in the air as he walked up behind Mr. Steele. He tapped the other man's shoulder, forcing him to turn around.

"Joshua, how nice to see you," Mr. Steele said, tucking his wallet into his back pocket.

"Not so nice, Mark. Not so nice at all."

"You're not still going on about this food stand business, are you?"

"I *am* still going on about it. I'm downright furious with you."

"Why is this my fault?" asked Mr. Steele.

"You knew I wanted a table, and you sold them out before even letting me know they were for sale. That, my dear friend, was not smart. My baked goods are the finest in River Heights. And this is the River Heights Festival."

Both men raised their voices to tense levels, shouting at each other, drawing a lot of attention from passersby. Mara enjoyed watching Mr. Steele be put in his place, but Chief McGinnis stood back for a bit, waiting to see if the men could settle their differences calmly. As I watched Mr. Andrews, I realized he was a clear suspect in this case. Although no one had seen him here at the carnival, Mrs. Gruen had mentioned how upset he was this morning, and it seemed his anger had not subsided. Especially toward Mr. Steele.

Finally Chief McGinnis stepped between the men, holding them apart as they continued to yell at each other. Mara told us she was going to check on the parade party to see how their decorations were coming along. Bess and I stood by the ticket booth, watching the men argue about the food stand.

"Do you think Mr. Andrews stole the money?" I asked Bess.

"It's possible, but unlikely," Bess said. "Why would he?"

"Not sure. We need to find Ned and ask him if he saw Mr. Andrews poking around this morning. It's the only way to know for sure if he's a true suspect. Someone would have seen him here. I know Mrs. Gruen saw him early this morning at his store."

"Nancy, do you think we'll ever find out who stole the money?" asked Bess, wiping her paint-covered hand on a towel.

"I'm not sure, Bess. Every time I think we get going in the right direction, something comes along and makes it more complicated."

"Right," she said. "Like the notes and the threat of sabotage."

"Exactly. And the scariest part of all is that I don't have any suspects for any of it—the notes or the money."

"You'll figure it out, Nancy. You always do."

"I hope so. We need to find George and Ned and

regroup because the parade is starting soon, and I have a feeling whatever happens next will happen right before the parade."

The men finally calmed down and walked away in opposite directions as Chief McGinnis still stood between them. I wasn't sure how hard Chief was looking into all the facts, or how closely he was scrutinizing alibis, but he certainly seemed to be making less headway on the case than I was. Then again, he didn't officially know I was heading up my own investigation, something he would never allow. I needed to keep focused on the facts and follow them wherever they led me. Mr. Steele and Mr. Andrews made my job more difficult with this feud they'd created and more than likely distracted Chief from the missing money.

Chief McGinnis looked at me with worried eyes, almost like he was asking me to help him solve this case as soon as possible. He smiled at me, and I smiled back. I couldn't help but read into his smile, *Please help me, Nancy, before something else happens.*

I looked back at him and thought, *I am trying, Chief. I am trying.*

BLACK SMUDGES REVEALED

The ticket booth had finally closed, sold out of tickets, as Ned helped shut it down and lock it up. His father, James Nickerson, helped too, keeping an eye on everyone else, making sure no one suspicious was hanging around the booth.

"Hello, Mr. Nickerson," I said. "It's wonderful to see you."

"Hello, Fancy Nancy," he said.

Bess and Ned and Mr. Nickerson all laughed when he said this.

"All right," I said, my hands out, halting conversation. "I have enough unanswered questions and mysteries floating around today. I don't need everyone calling me that name all day long."

"Sorry, Nancy," Ned said.

"Yeah, sorry, Nancy," said Bess.

"You know," Mr. Nickerson said, "back in my days as a hard-hitting investigative reporter in Washington, a nickname given by friends and family was a sign of loyalty. Maybe you should embrace your new name?"

"Not at all. Everyone knows how much I hate that name, and I will find out who is behind it. If it's the last thing I do." I couldn't believe how much I sounded like Chief McGinnis and his clichéd and cheesy one-liners. I almost sounded like a villain. This nickname thing was bothering me, but I had to keep my focus on the case I was working on.

"Well, I hope you find out who took the money first," Ned said.

"Yeah, these were some serious allegations I heard about," Mr. Nickerson said. "That's, why I'm here." Mr. Nickerson was the publisher of the *River Heights Bugle*, our local newspaper. "Like my newspaper's motto, I am committed to truth in journalism. We must find the thief, so Ned's innocence will be proven." He seemed a little too interested and excited about the missing money.

"We will find the thief, Mr. Nickerson," I said. "I'm working on a few angles right now."

"Absolutely," Bess said. "We're waiting for George, who might have a solid lead for us." I couldn't believe Bess had blurted out the fact that we might have some secret evidence. This was exactly the type of thing that Mr. Nickerson was waiting to hear. We needed to protect our information, so as not to scare off potential perpetrators. By telling Mr. Nickerson that we had evidence, we might as well have asked him to write an article about the case itself and publish it in the newspaper tomorrow.

I turned to Ned. "I have a question for you."

"What is it?" he said.

"Do you remember seeing Mr. Andrews poking around the ticket booth this morning? I know you saw Deirdre, Josh, and Mara, but did you by any chance see Mr. Andrews?"

"Nope. Why?" Ned asked.

"Do you really think Joshua Andrews had something to do with this?" Mr. Nickerson asked, concerned and inquisitive. "I would find him hard to believe as a suspect."

"I'm not sure," I said. "I keep thinking I'm on the right track, but my leads are drying up faster than a drought." I wanted to steer the conversation away from the case, but Mr. Nickerson was too interested to let it go.

I stared at Bess for a while, hoping to get her attention. She finally looked over at me, and I widened my eyes as if to say, *We have to leave and get away from them right now.*

However, Bess must have misinterpreted my facial expression, as she continued to give away our information on the case.

"George is working on analyzing one of the notes as we speak," she said. "We might have a black smudge of some kind that could direct us toward a new suspect."

"Black smudge?" Mr. Nickerson repeated. "Interesting."

"Don't get any ideas, Mr. Nickerson," I said. "You are not writing any article on this mystery. We're only speculating on possible information right now. All our initial suspects seem to have alibis. Except Mr. Andrews, which is why I want Ned here to find out more."

"What do you need me to do?" asked Ned. "I want to help you clear my name. I will do anything it takes."

"Okay. Sounds good. I need you to buddy up to Mr. Andrews and find out why he's so upset with Mark Steele. They had an argument earlier, and it seemed pretty serious," I said. I already knew why the two men were mad at each other, but my goal in asking Ned to do this served several purposes. It kept him and his father busy and only directed them to information I already had. I wanted to stay in charge of the investigation and not have too many people going off on their own, trying to help.

"I saw that," Mr. Nickerson said. "When I was parking my car, I saw Chief McGinnis breaking up their argument and stepping between them."

"It got a little heated," I said.

"Any possible motives for the fight?" Mr. Nickerson asked.

"Maybe," I said, still trying to be vague and keep Mr. Nickerson subdued.

"I'm on it," Ned said. "Leave it to me. I'm your man for the job. I'll get to the bottom of it." It was cute, seeing him excited about his mission, although I already knew what information he would find out. "Do you think we have a shot at recovering the money?"

"The sooner we can isolate the thief, the better shot we have at finding the money. So we need to work fast," I said. "You get going on your mission, Ned."

Ned and his father finished closing down the ticket booth and headed off into the carnival to find Mr.

Andrews. Maybe Mr. Nickerson would use some of his old-school reporting techniques to uncover more evidence for us than I expected. In any case, they were no longer hounding me for information, and Bess couldn't give away any more of our evidence.

Bess grabbed my arm and shook it, pointing toward the school as George ran like a track star out of the building, headed right toward us.

"Look," Bess said. "If she doesn't slow down, she's going to run right into us. You know how incredibly uncoordinated she can be sometimes."

"Bess," I said, shocked. "Be nice!"

"She's my cousin," said Bess. "I can say she's uncoordinated and get away with it. Now if *you* called her uncoordinated, then there'd be a problem."

I knew immediately that George had found something on the note. She had been gone for a while, testing out her new science toy, but now she was a track star, bolting from the building toward us. I could tell by the look on her face—surprise and glee—that she was excited and couldn't wait to get to us. George finally slowed down and took a minute to catch her breath.

"Why are so many people running today?" I asked. "George, Bess, Mara, Mr. Steele. Everyone is running everywhere. You would think we were all running from a fire."

"I found . . ." George started to speak, but couldn't finish her sentence.

"Please spit it out," Bess said. "We know that you found something good."

"I . . . found . . . something," said George. Then she continued, "The note."

"That's rather vague," Bess said. "Please give us more than that."

"What was it?" I asked. "What did you find out? What is it about the note? Come on, George. Take a few big breaths."

"I can't . . . just . . . follow . . . come with me," George said. She turned and walked back toward the school, huffing and puffing. Her excitement about whatever she'd found was overwhelming her to the point where she couldn't communicate at all. Bess and I followed her back across the parking lot to the school, hoping that whatever George had found would be helpful to the case. The culprit was having a field day sending out clues that drove the investigation in all directions.

"What, we're not going to run back to the school now?" asked Bess. "You looked like a track star." Bess struck a pose, making fun of her cousin.

We all exchanged looks and laughed. Bess knew she could push our buttons to alleviate the tension that was building up all around us. The longer we went without solving the crimes—the notes, the missing money—the more people depended on us to vindicate them and prove they weren't suspects.

We finally reached the school, trying not to let anyone see us sneaking around, especially Mr. Steele. No one was allowed to be in the school on the weekends unsupervised, so we needed to be extraordinarily careful. All the teachers seemed to be back at the carnival. The coast was clear. I counted to three before signaling Bess and George to duck inside the school door. We snuck down the hallway to the biology lab, where George had her new toy set up next to a microscope. We closed the door behind us. I placed a piece of black construction paper over the window in the door to shield us from any possible passersby.

On one of the lab tables, under the microscope, was the latest blue note from the fro-yo stand.

"What is this monstrosity?" Bess asked, pointing at George's new gadget next to the microscope.

The machine looked like a toaster. It was silver with black buttons and a door that was closed, but could be opened up on the side like a drawbridge. George's bedroom was filled from floor to ceiling with devices like this one. She loved the latest in technology, especially anything that came with a computer chip.

"It's an EDCS," George said.

"Sounds like some kind of disease," said Bess. "Am I going to catch the flu or something?"

"It stands for Element Disintegration Chemistry Set," I said. "I think. I could be wrong. George, why do all your science toys have extremely long names?"

"It's my new high-tech NASA-developed Element Disintegration Chemistry Set." She looked annoyed at Bess, but was also a little bit annoyed at me. We were always teasing her about her hobby, but really only because we weren't interested in the technological or scientific. "Trust me," she said, "when I say that, Bess, you will not catch the flu from this device."

"How does it work?" Bess asked.

George took out a tiny test tube from a recently opened box. She dropped a sliver of the note to the bottom before adding a drop of inky-looking fluid and an ounce or so of water on top, then mixed it all together by swirling the tube. She held it high in the air for us to see. The paper and solution didn't look any different to me, but held back any judgment until George finished her presentation.

"I took a small piece of the note that had the smudge on it, mixed it with a special solution compound, and then set it in the circular wheel of the EDCS." George opened the drawbridge door to the toasterlike machine. Inside was a wheel, where she placed the test tube before closing up the door. "Next

I set it on high, and it spins the sample around under high temperatures." She punched a black button on the machine as it made a whirring sound. "Then it analyzes and computes the individual elements in the solution and prints out a report, telling you what it could be. Sometimes it's specific. Sometimes it's general. Depends on the complexity of the sample."

"How long does it take?" I asked.

"Seconds," said George. At that moment the machine began to print out a tiny piece of paper. George ripped it off the machine and handed it to me. "I've run this test three times now, and it comes back the same every time."

"What did you find, George?" I asked. "Something good, I hope. We need a good lead." I took the paper from her and began to read it.

"Look in the microscope first," George said, pointing to the microscope.

I leaned over the microscope and peered down the lens at the blue note. I wasn't exactly sure what I was supposed to be looking at. The letters in the note were very large, like in an oversize print book for old people with bad eyes. The note looked like it was in high resolution. At the edges were smears or smudges of something dark, darker than the pen used to write the note. I moved the paper around to examine every inch of it.

"What I am looking for?" I asked. I had a feeling it had to do with the smudges.

"Look at the smudges," George said. "I compared them to the ink used in the letters and they don't match. So the smudges are a special kind of ink. Look at the results again."

I stepped away from the microscope and reread the printout analysis. Bess stepped up to the microscope and looked down too.

The printout read:

Commercial ink compound
Example: Ballaster Ink

"What does this mean exactly?" I asked.

"According to my research and my EDCS, it's no ink from any kind of printer or copier or pen. I thought for a while maybe it was grease or oil from a car."

"Which might point to Deirdre's boyfriend, Josh," Bess said. "Because of the car accident."

"But the ink is too light," George pointed out. "The ink in the note is special too. Apparently, that comes from a fountain pen. It's an ink source that you have to special order online to be able to refill the pen."

"So the smudges are also ink?"

"Yes," said George.

"But not fountain pen ink," Bess said.

"Correct," said George.

"Other than pens and printers, what else uses a lot of ink that is highly specialized?" I asked out loud, brainstorming.

"I don't know. My new machine didn't say. Just said it was a commercial ink generally purchased in large quantities," George said.

"And what did you find out about this Ballaster Ink?" I asked.

"Nothing," George said. "I called the local office supply store, but they didn't carry it. I asked to speak with the store manager, and she'd never heard of it."

"Back to square one," Bess said.

"Not necessarily," I said. "This is good work, George. We know that whoever wrote this note uses a fountain pen with ink that has to be special ordered. The person also has access to a very specific kind of commercial ink called Ballaster Ink."

"How is any of this helpful?" asked Bess.

"It helps us to build a profile. It helps us to look for clues. Who do we know who uses a fountain pen? Who do we know has ink on their fingers all the time? These are questions we should be asking ourselves. Really good work," I said.

Suddenly Bess's cell phone rang, and all three of us jumped. We desperately tried to quiet our laughter, so that Bess could answer her call. I shushed us all enough with one of my hands over George's mouth. She had the most trouble controlling her laughter. Bess answered her call, still laughing herself.

"What?" she asked, her laughter falling away fast. "What happened? Why can't you tell me? Okay, I'll be right there." She hung up and turned to us.

"Who was it?" George asked.

"Spit it out, Bess. What happened?" I chimed in.

"I'm not sure," she said. "That was Mara. She wants to see me right away."

"Why?" I asked.

"I don't know. All she said was to meet her in the girls' bathroom near the gym immediately. She told me not to tell anyone. She said it was an emergency."

"She didn't say why?" asked George.

"No," Bess said.

"Did you hear anything else?" I asked.

"I heard other voices in the background," Bess said.

"What did they sound like? What were they saying?" I asked.

"They sounded like they were crying."

We stood there for a minute in silence, mulling over all the erroneous leads and clues we had collected all day. Everything kept running us in circles until we all looked up at the same time. We knew suddenly what that call from Mara was about.

At the same time we all said, "The parade."

George packed up her machine as Bess and I put away the microscope and took the note with us. We ran out of the school and across the parking lot, passing in front of the ticket booth, heading toward the gymnasium. The parade was starting soon, and the girls' bathroom was where the girls were getting dressed and doing their makeup.

As we made our way through the crowd, I saw Mr. Nickerson and Ned sitting on a picnic bench with my dad. All three of us slowed down, so as not to draw attention to ourselves. We didn't want them to suspect that there were any problems. We needed to stop, say hello, and be cool and calm, so we could slip away to the gymnasium. I hoped that George could be smooth enough not to give away any of our leads.

"I'll stop and talk to them," I said. "Bess, you go on to the gym and call me as soon as you find out what's happened." I looked at George. "George, you okay?"

"Yeah, why?" she asked.

"Just checking. Let's try and keep as much information about this whole thing as private as possible for the time being, okay?"

Bess ran past everyone, waving briefly, as George and I stopped at the picnic bench.

"Fancy Nancy," Dad said, slapping Mr. Nickerson's back. Mr. Nickerson had obviously told Dad about how much I hated that name, and they were both having a good laugh about it now.

"Dad," I said. "Hey. What's everyone up to?" Even though I was worried about George giving away information, I tried to be cool and calm myself, but everything I did or said came out awkward and weird.

George leaned toward me and whispered, "You sound so awkward and weird right now. Stop acting weird. They're going to find out. Remember what you said to me?"

"Ned," I said, "did you get a chance to talk to Mr. Andrews?"

"We did," said Mr. Nickerson. "Just a little while ago, actually." He was still pushing himself into this mystery. He really wanted to be a part of its resolution.

"It wasn't him," Dad said.

"What?" I asked, looking at Ned.

"Our father units took it upon themselves to insert themselves into our unsolved mystery," Ned said. He laughed. "I tried to control them, but they think they're professional detectives or something."

"How do you know it wasn't him?" I asked.

"Well, your dad said that Mrs. Gruen went to the bakery early in the morning, around eight a.m. or so," Ned said. "If that's correct, it's the same time I arrived at the ticket booth. By the time I opened up, and between all my visitors—Deirdre, Josh, and Mara—there is no way he closed the bakery, drove over here, stole the cash box, went back to the store, and opened it back up, all without ever being seen."

"I was at the bakery this morning too. Around eight thirty," Mr. Nickerson said. "Joshua seemed irritated, but not mad enough to steal money."

"He's apparently mad at Mark Steele for not saving a food booth for him to sell his baked goods. He spent all last night baking for today, but found out this morning that all the booth space had been rented."

I looked at George and shook my head. "This is bad," I said, speaking softly so only she could hear me. "We just might be back at square one."

"Oh honey," said Dad, walking over and hugging me. "I know that look anywhere." He pinched my cheek. "Don't you worry. Everything is going to be okay. Something else will pop up that will trip this thief up so the authorities can catch him or her. The chief has everything under control."

"I feel like I'm on the right track, though," I said. "I

just need some more time. Whoever is doing all this will make mistakes, and it's just a matter of time."

"Nancy, we should get going," George said. "You know. To meet Bess."

Now George was being super weird.

"Right. Well, we have to run. Bess needs our help in the gym," I said.

"Where were you girls coming from?" Mr. Nickerson said. "It looked like you were leaving the school." He pointed behind us, across the parking lot, to the back entrance of the school.

"We found something on one of the notes and had to examine it closer. We needed to use the biology lab," I said.

"What did you find out, honey?" asked Dad.

"One of the notes had a special kind of ink on it that isn't carried in office supply stores. But no one seems to know what it is or where it's used," I said.

"Ink?" Ned said. "What kind of ink?"

"The brand name is called Ballaster Ink," I said.

Mr. Nickerson's jaw dropped open. "Ballaster Ink?" he asked. "On the note?"

"A smudge in the corner," I said.

"Ballaster Ink is a brand that a lot of independent publishers use for printing their newspapers. It's less expensive than the ink that the national newspapers use, which allows them to be more competitive. We use Ballaster Ink for the *River Heights Bugle*."

"Our thief is a newspaper reader," I said.

"A heavy reader at that. Most people read a newspaper, then wash their hands right away. Someone who was careless enough to leave a smudge of this ink on the note probably reads a lot of these type of newspapers and must have forgotten to wash their hands after they finished one," Mr. Nickerson said.

"Excellent investigative reporting skills, Dad," Ned said.

"I still got it," said Mr. Nickerson, breathing on his nails and rubbing them on his chest, showing off.

My cell phone buzzed in my pocket. It was a text message from Bess. GET HERE RIGHT NOW, the text read. Then it continued, WE HAVE ANOTHER SABOTAGE.

7

ANOTHER SABOTAGE

George and I excused ourselves from the picnic table and headed to the gymnasium. As we arrived, we saw the float parked out front, decorated now with flowers and signage for the River Heights Celebration parade. The throne was covered in glitter and flowers, with a bouquet resting for Lexi to hold as she waved to everyone. I had to admit that it looked beautiful and grand, but something kept nagging at me—why did someone want all of this to end? Someone was going through a lot of trouble to sabotage the parade and the carnival and the food court, like they wanted it all to disappear. Each person on our list of suspects certainly had a motive to sabotage a portion of the carnival, but not one person seemed to have the motive to be responsible for all the sabotage. And the closer it got in the day toward the start of the parade, the more nervous I got that we were never going to catch the criminal behind all of this. Worse still, I was afraid something bigger and more dangerous was going to happen.

We needed another clue, and we needed it right away.

When we entered the gymnasium, we found Bess standing inside, pacing back and forth in front of a trophy case. I had seen her worried and scared many times before, but never like this. She looked genuinely upset. She kept running her hand through her hair and sighing heavily.

"Bess," George said. "What's wrong?"

"This is getting a little too real," she said. "Way too real. Like, dangerous."

"Are you okay?" I asked.

"I'm fine." She paused, like she was replaying her answer in her head and didn't agree with it. Then she continued, "No. I change that. I am not fine. I am very nervous that things are getting out of control here and that there might be nothing any of us can do about it."

"What happened?" I asked.

"The bathroom was to be the dressing room for all the girls involved with the float. Everyone would meet there and get ready for the parade together," she said. "Then Mara called me. When I arrived, when everyone arrived, we were all met with what you are about to see inside."

We all looked at the bathroom door. George took a step back from it.

"Who's in there?" George asked.

"Lexi has locked herself inside one of the bathroom stalls, and Mara is in there on the phone with different people. She keeps calling people. Other than that, it's just me and now you guys."

"We're here now," I said. "Let's go in and handle this situation like we've been handling everything else today. There's nothing to be afraid of here."

"Did you guys find out anything from Ned?" Bess asked.

"We did, actually. Apparently, Ballaster Ink is used by independent newspaper presses. It's cheaper than the ink the national newspapers use."

"What does this mean?" asked Bess.

"We're looking for someone who reads a lot," George said.

"That's good, because whoever is behind all of this certainly likes to write a lot. Between the notes and what you're about to see, you'll know what I mean," Bess said.

She knocked on the bathroom door before pushing it open.

Inside, white and light blue feathers mixed with shredded fabric covered the floor and walls. The shreds looked like they'd been torn and ripped in a frenzy. I kicked through the feathers and cloth on the floor and saw on the wall that the words CANCEL THE RIVER HEIGHTS CARNIVAL had been written all over in a black marker. On the mirrors, words were written too. STOP. BEWARE. CANCEL THE PARADE. The entire room was torn apart and graffiitied in threats. Soft cries came from inside one of the stalls—Lexi. Mara was in the corner on her cell phone.

"What is all this?" George asked. "What happened here?"

"The feathers are from Lexi's crown, and the white fabric is her dress," Bess said. "They ripped up her dress and destroyed the crown."

"I don't understand." George walked around, stopping briefly to scoop up a handful and inspect it. "Why would someone go through all this trouble?"

"Look at the warnings on the wall," I said. "They wanted the parade to end. They want the carnival to end. They want it all to be shut down."

"Whoever it is came in here after Mara dropped off

the crown and dress, but before any of the students. They must have been watching Mara, following her closely. They came in here, found the crown, broke it, and tore up the dress," Bess said. "Lexi now has no dress for the parade, and her crown is destroyed."

"Why was the dress here in the first place?" I asked. "Why would Mara leave it unattended?"

"Mara dropped it off for Lexi, who was finishing up at the fro-yo stand before coming over here to get ready," Bess explained. "She left it here unattended to save time. She honestly didn't think anything would happen to it."

"This is very strange," I said. "We need to let Chief McGinnis know about all this. We have to stop the parade. It isn't safe for it to go on as planned. We need to listen to these threats for once and cancel the parade."

"That's what I tried telling Mara, but she won't listen to me," said Bess, pointing to Mara in the corner, digging through her Prada purse. "You would think someone with exceptional taste in accessories and expensive purses like that would want to distance herself from this madness, but she won't back down. She wants the parade to happen more than ever right now."

"Let me go and talk to her," I said. "Maybe she'll listen to third-party reasoning in all this parade madness."

I walked over to Mara and waited for her to finish one of her many phone calls. She looked absolutely focused, terribly fierce and aggressive. She was obviously determined that this type of sabotage was not going to ruin all her parade planning.

"Mara, can we speak privately about this?" I said, pointing to the closed stall door where Lexi still whimpered inside. I then pointed to the bathroom door, gesturing for us to leave.

"You want me to go outside with you?" she asked bluntly. "Because we can't talk in front of your little friends?" She was very curt with me.

"Yes," I finally said. "Let's leave these girls alone for a few minutes. I would like to discuss what is happening and what you think your next move should be. But I would prefer to do it quietly and privately, if you don't mind."

We walked across the room and left the bathroom and the mess behind.

"Nancy, I really don't think this has anything to do with you," Mara said. "This is a grown-up problem. Not a fro-yo stand problem."

I took a breath and let her shortsightedness wash over me before I decided to let her in on my investigation. She didn't realize how much I knew already. She didn't know that I had been piecing this investigation together all day. I wasn't even sure she was aware that the notes had been targeting everyone, not just her. I decided, in the interest of full disclosure, that I was going to tip my hand to her and tell her everything I knew, so that she could see I actually was more qualified to be a part of the solution than she was willing to allow.

"Mara, please listen," I said. "I'm afraid your parade sabotage situation has a lot to do with the other crimes happening today."

"Like what?" she said again in a blunt and curt tone. "What other crimes? The missing money? You're being ridiculous."

"Yes, the stolen money. The mysterious threatening notes. Now the torn dress and the graffiti on the walls," I said. "This is a very delicate and dangerous situation. For you. For Lexi. For everyone in the parade. We really need to cancel it, or I'm afraid something worse will happen."

"Delicate and dangerous situation, huh?" she said. "Quite big words for Fancy Nancy. I appreciate your sweet concern, but everything will be okay. Why don't you leave the parade and the nice little love letter written on the walls in there up to adults?"

"Who told you to call me that name?" I asked. "Who said to call me Fancy Nancy? I want to know."

"Look," she said, stepping back. "I appreciate your

concern and your assistance here. Really. I do. And I appreciate that you and your friends are having an exciting adventure solving mysteries. I remember doing the same thing when I was your age. But I doubt that the notes and the money and all of that in there," she said pointing to the bathroom, "have anything to do with each other. My guess is that some girl is upset that she wasn't selected to be on the float, and this is her revenge."

"Okay," I said. "I understand your reservations about letting me and my friends help, but we found something on one of the notes. A smudge. It's a certain type of ink. Now if you let me look at what's left of the dress and I find any black smudges, then I would be willing to bet that whoever is responsible for the notes is tied to your parade sabotage too. We would actually have evidence linking the crimes together."

"Fine," she said. "But then I'm calling Chief McGinnis."

"You should," I said. "This sabotage has crossed the line from silly to sinister. We need to stop the parade immediately."

We walked back into the bathroom just in time to see Bess speaking to Lexi through the bathroom stall, begging her to come out. George knelt on the floor, sifting through the confetti of feathers and cloth. She held a tattered rag in her hands.

"What's that?" I asked.

"What's left of the dress," Mara said.

George held it up to show me; it was no bigger than a kitchen hand towel. "Look," she said, tossing it to me. "Look at the edge—black smudges."

"You have got to be kidding me," said Mara, looking over my shoulder.

As I held it up to the light, sure enough, there at the edge was a smudge. I flipped the piece of cloth over in my hands and found several more smudges. This was our link, tying it all together—the money, the notes, the dress.

"Well, maybe it's from the black marker they used on the walls," Mara said.

I took my finger and rubbed on the smudges. Each one smeared and blended more into the fabric. "The black smudges on the fabric smear. This is not permanent ink. George," I said, "try the ink on the walls."

George grabbed a paper towel from the dispenser and ran it under cold water in the sink. She placed the paper towel on the wall where the words were written and scrubbed against the black marker words. The black marker did not smear.

"The wall was vandalized with permanent marker. This," I said, shaking the cloth, "is ink just like on the notes. We're dealing with the same person here. The notes and the dress and the missing money—all the crimes were committed by the same person."

Just then Lexi's former boyfriend, Scott Sears, opened the door a crack and asked if Lexi was in there. Even though Lexi hadn't said a word in response to Mara, Bess, or even me about the sabotage, except to weep quietly in the stall, as soon as she heard Scott's voice, she flung open the door and ran straight for him.

"Scott! Oh, Scott! You're here. You really came for me."

"I ran here as soon as I heard something was wrong," he said.

Bess, who has had a crush on Scott, smiled when she heard his voice too. I shook my head at her and whispered, "Forget about it."

"What happened?" Scott asked Lexi as she threw her arms around his neck. "I heard that you needed some help in here. You okay?"

"Well," Bess said, stepping forward, "it seems someone doesn't want the parade to happen. They ripped up Lexi's dress and her crown and left us lovely little notes on the walls." She pointed to everything.

"Really?" he said. "Well, everyone outside is expecting to see the parade. They're all lined up and waiting for it to begin. Is it still happening? Will the parade still take place?"

"Not quite," Lexi said, still crying. "It's probably going to be canceled. I don't even have anything to wear!"

"Oh, that reminds me," he said, reaching for something in his pocket. "I found this taped to the door of the bathroom when I knocked."

It was another blue note. I grabbed it right away and examined the edges. More black smudges. Bess and George saw them too. We knew what was inside before I even opened it.

I WARNED YOU.
THIS IS YOUR LAST CHANCE.
CANCEL THE PARADE.
OR ELSE.

"Or else what?" said Mara.

"Or else expect the worst possible outcome," I said. "This is what I've been trying to explain to you. Whoever is doing this is not joking around. They're serious. They mean business. And if you go forward with this parade, you can absolutely be sure that something will go wrong. Possibly, even horribly so."

"I am not going to let this joker terrorize me with his silly notes and scissors cutting up our clothes." Mara slid her Prada purse up onto her shoulder. "There's nothing to be afraid of, Lexi. There's nothing to be so concerned about, Nancy. Everything is fine."

"I'm so scared, Mara," Lexi said.

"Don't be," said Mara. "We are going out there and having the parade as scheduled. You are going to wave and the crowd is going to love you and we are all going to have a great time."

"I don't have a crown or even a white dress to wear," Lexi said.

"I actually have an extra dress in my trunk. If a lifetime of planning these types of events has taught me anything, it is to always have backups. Backups of everything. Makeup. Shoes. Dresses. Everything. I'll go and grab them." Mara pushed past Scott and exited the gymnasium.

"Backups of everything except a backup plan," I said softly to myself, quickly strategizing my next move.

"This is all so crazy," Scott said. "Someone needs to tell Chief McGinnis. He's right outside, waiting to see the parade like everyone else. I'm going to bring him here to show him what's happening." Scott left too, right behind Mara.

"Nancy, Bess, George, thank you so much for coming down here. After everything that happened yesterday, it just means so much to me that you all were willing to help out again," Lexi said.

"Of course," said George.

"Don't mention it," I said. "But we need to tell Chief about this and make sure you don't get on that float. Something really bad is going to happen. The notes have been threatening the parade all day. If the parade goes on, something *will* happen. This," I said, throwing a fistful of white and light blue feathers in the air, "is just the beginning. You can bet that there'll be more to come."

"I know," said Lexi. "But no one is going to convince Mara. You see how stubborn and determined she can be about all this. Trust me. This is what makes her so happy. She looks forward to it every year. I really don't think she'll change her mind."

"Change my mind about what?" Mara said, walking through the door with another dress in her hand.

"Canceling the parade," Bess said.

"It's the safe thing to do," said George.

"It's the *right* thing to do," I said.

"Please," Lexi said. "Please. And we don't even have to cancel. We could just reschedule."

"I've had some time to think this over," she said, leaning her hands on the sink, looking into the threats written across the mirrors. "I organize and run this parade every year. You know we've had every imaginable problem happen in years past threatening to cancel the parade? Girls have had the flu. Flat tires on their cars when they left their houses in the morning. Flat tires on the float. One year the key broke off in the lock to the band room with every instrument still inside. And every year we find a way to pull it together. We find a way to pull through. In all these years, we have never had to cancel. And this year will not be any different. The parade will go on as scheduled. And that is final."

Lexi looked white as a bedsheet. Her hands trembled, and tears continued to run down her cheeks. I walked over to her and held her hands.

"Lexi, it's all going to be okay. I promise," I said.

"Nancy," Lexi said, "will you ride on the float with me?"

"No, I won't," I said, "because the parade is not happening. I'm not giving up just yet."

Chief McGinnis knocked on the bathroom door. "Ladies, would you all please explain to me what in the heck is happening in there? There are all kinds of crazy rumors flying around."

Mara opened the door, revealing to him the vandalism inside. The feathers and fabric and graffiti. We all stood there with our arms crossed as he surveyed the room. His facial expression was exactly as befuddled and dumbfounded as I had expected it to be.

"What is this?" he asked. "Scott said you all were in danger."

"Scott is overreacting. We're not in any danger," said Mara. "Just another silly prank by some kids. Nothing that we can't handle."

"Do we need to cancel the parade?" he asked.

"Yes," I said. "Chief, we absolutely need to cancel the parade."

"Nancy Drew, why is it that every time there's been a problem today, you and your friends are around?" Chief McGinnis mused. "I'm beginning to believe that *you* have something to do with all this. The missing money this morning. The shredded feathers in here. And if this isn't your handiwork, I would consider the fact that someone is making it seem awfully convenient that you're always hanging around when a crime is committed."

"Chief," Mara said, "Nancy and her friends are okay. They've been a great big help here. They had nothing to do with this at all. It's probably a bitter girl who was not selected to participate this year."

"Are you sure?" he asked. "Because I can drag them out of here. Send them home. Banish them from the carnival altogether."

"They're fine," she said. "But they have an interesting theory about the notes that have been found around the carnival yesterday and today. And they think whoever is writing the notes has also stolen the money."

"Really?" he asked.

"Show Chief what you girls showed me," she said.

"Well, Chief, I wouldn't presume to be as good a detective as you. I mean, you are a professional, after all," I said. "And I'm just a teenage girl."

Bess and George laughed, not to be mean, but because we had solved so many crimes over the years, and when Chief was involved we would surely solve them before he would and end up giving him all the credit for solving a mystery that had essentially been solved by us.

"Let's all leave Lexi and Mrs. Stanfield alone to finish getting ready for the parade, and afterward, why don't you and I sit down and discuss the notes and stolen money," he suggested. "I would also love to hear your whereabouts this morning. Just so I can rule you out as a suspect. You know the drill, right?"

"Absolutely, Chief," I said. "Mrs. Gruen and my dad can vouch for my whereabouts. I believe police refer to it as an airtight alibi, but you're right, let's talk after the parade."

All three of us—George, Bess, and I—left Lexi in the bathroom to get dressed, but right before the door closed it was opened again.

"Nancy!" Lexi called out.

"Don't worry, Lexi," I said.

"It's all going to be okay," said George.

"Please ride on the float with me," Lexi said. "Don't let me get on that thing by myself."

"I will be on the float with you," I said. "Bess is checking the alterations on the float one last time. George will be watching us from the crowd, and officer Joe Rees will be driving the float. You will be well protected and guarded."

"Thank you, Nancy," she said. "I'm sorry for any mean things I ever said about you behind your back. You really are a good friend." Then she closed the door.

This was the first time it occurred to me that whoever had started the nickname of "Fancy Nancy" was actually trying to get back at me. The name was an attempt to drive me crazy, just the way that someone who didn't like me would want. Lexi's honesty was very real, so I knew she wasn't the one who'd started the name, but it could very well have been someone in her circle of fro-yo friends. I needed to take a closer look at my enemies to find out the truth.

8

RIVER HEIGHTS CELEBRATION PARADE, FINALLY

Outside the gymnasium, the parade was about to begin.

"Finally," a man said, calling from the street. He stood with his family, excited about the parade. He tapped his two kids on the shoulders, getting their attention, and pointed in our direction. One by one the crowd saw the parade gathering and about to begin, and they cheered and clapped, preparing for us to pass by them on the street.

The band lined up in front of the float, testing their instruments, running scales and adjusting their River Heights High School uniforms and fuzzy hats. The crowds continued to line up along the street, waving banners and eating their carnival food—big pretzels, fro-yo, funnel cakes, hot dogs, caramel popcorn, and cotton candy. Little kids blew whistles and danced in the street, impatient for the parade to begin.

Dad and Mr. Nickerson stood together, with Ned nearby. They wore concerned looks on their faces, but they didn't know about the torn dress and graffiti threats, so hopefully they weren't as scared as Lexi. Frankly, at that point, I was fairly scared myself. The whole day had been one crime after another. I knew something was going to happen. We all did, but neither the chief nor Mara would listen to us, so all we could do was be prepared.

Mr. Steele and Chief McGinnis waited near the entrance to the gymnasium, overseeing the last-minute lineup and roll call of the parade participants. Mr. Steele seemed distracted by Mara Stanfield; he didn't take his eyes off her while she fixed Lexi's hair and adjusted her new dress. Chief McGinnis kept one eye on the group of us. I couldn't believe he thought I might be the one behind the notes and stolen money. On one hand, I understood where he was coming from; it was true that every time a crime was committed, I was there. But he knew me better than that. I looked forward to proving my innocence to him, not that I needed to in any real sense, but if that was what it was going to take to get him to listen to the evidence that George, Bess, and I had uncovered today, then so be it.

Deirdre and Josh held hands and sat on the curb. I wondered if his parents had found out about his car accident yet, or if the driver of the other car had found his note.

"Nancy, I'm really scared," said Lexi, standing next to me as we climbed the stairs of the float. Lexi took her place on the throne, sitting among the flowers and glitter.

"I know you're scared, Lexi, but look," I said. "Bess will be on the float with us too. I'll sit on the front of the float, and she'll be right behind the throne. This way we can keep an eye on everything in front of us and everything behind us."

"Where will Officer Rees be?" she asked.

"He will be in the driver's seat at the very back, monitoring the speed."

"And George?" Lexi asked.

"George is going to walk along the parade route next to us. She'll keep an eye on the spectators. You're well surrounded, Lexi." I looked up as Mara Stanfield clapped her hands for us all to get in our positions. "Also, if you see or hear anything that doesn't seem right, just tell Bess or me and we'll take care of it."

Lexi smiled and sat back. As she did, the crowd began to cheer and clap again. The band played one of their songs and marched in perfect time with one another. The float engine rumbled as Officer Rees turned the ignition and moved the float into position behind the band. Lexi sat on her throne, waving and smiling as flowers were thrown from the crowd and landed on the deck of the float.

Before George and Bess got into position, I pulled them aside for a last-minute pep talk and game plan.

"Okay, girls. We all know that something is going to happen during the parade, so let's keep our eyes sharp."

"Are we sure something will happen?" asked Bess.

"What do you mean?" I asked.

"I just think we've spent so much time on the stolen money and the notes," Bess said, "that I'm wondering if we might be making this into a bigger issue than it actually is, you know. Like maybe we're creating this drama."

"There has been way too much evidence," George said. "Nancy is right. Something is going to happen, and we have to be alert. Lexi is only following through on this parade because Mara wouldn't cancel it."

"Bess," I said, "I totally understand your concerns. So if you feel like I'm overreacting and don't want to have a part in any of this, please feel free to sit back with the spectators and enjoy the parade."

"George," said Bess, "do you think all these

incidents are linked together somehow?" I was sure she was asking her cousin this question as a way to get reassurance.

"I do," George said. "I believe we've been right all day long. I believe everything is connected and that we're close to finding out who is behind it all."

"Okay. I'm in," said Bess. "I'm just nervous and want everything and everyone to be safe."

"Which is why we're going to ride along with the float. Bess, you double-check all the alterations one last time to make sure nothing new has changed. When you're ready, sit behind the throne and watch the float from behind."

"You got it, Nancy," she said.

"George, you walk on the ground next to the float. Keep an eye on the crowd and make sure no one and nothing comes at us from the sides."

"No problem, Nancy," she said.

"Let's stay in touch by cell phones too. Call me if you see something peculiar. And if you do see something, whatever you do, don't let Mara, Chief McGinnis, or Lexi know about it. Let's try and handle it ourselves."

Bess walked around the float, testing the railings again, and the platform in front of the throne. The paint was still wet, but that wasn't too big of an issue, as it was mostly covered by the decorations.

Everything seemed to be safe and as it had been this morning when it was delivered. Bess gave us the thumbs-up and settled in behind the throne as I sat in the front. George took up her position next to us on the ground, and we all waited for the parade to begin its route through River Heights.

The banner above Lexi's throne flapped in the slight breeze. It read:

Lexi Claremont
Daughter of River Heights

My cell phone rang almost right away. I pulled it out and saw that it was George, who was walking to my left and was at the very back of the float.

"Nancy," she said.

"Everything okay?"

"It's hard to see into the crowd. There are too many people. And most of them have balloons and foam fingers and food. It's going to be difficult to see anyone coming at us."

"Don't worry. Just do the best you can and keep in touch with me," I said. My phone beeped—it was Bess calling on the other line. I put George on hold and clicked over to Bess.

"What's up, Bess?" I said.

"Everything okay with George?"

"Yeah, I think so. She's having a tough time dealing with the crowd. Too much movement and too many people. Why?"

"I saw someone on the other side, someone I've never seen before. He looked suspicious to me. You know how we know pretty much everyone in River Heights, or at least know what they look like?"

"Yeah."

"Well, I don't know this guy."

"One second," I said, as I clicked on conference call and connected all three of us together.

"Bess. George," I said. "Are you all on the line?"

"Here," said Bess.

"Here," said George.

"Great. Bess, repeat to George what you just said to me. What do you see?" I asked.

"There's a man walking along the sidewalk with the float. He's behind the crowd lined along the curb, and he's walking in step with the float. I've never seen him before. Not a local."

"Which side?" asked George.

"Right side," Bess said.

George ran behind the float to the right side and scoured the crowd for a man walking with the float in the crowd, but she didn't see anyone. She walked right up to the crowd, then through the crowd. She passed a group of kids dancing to the band's music and pushed her way through a sea of white and blue balloons. She reached the sidewalk behind the parade watchers and was now observing the float from the spectators' position. She spun around, looking in all directions.

"I don't see anyone strange," she said. "Just kids and parents."

"He's by the tree now. He keeps staring at the float," Bess said.

George looked toward the next tree and finally saw the man.

"The man in the red cap?" George asked.

"Yes," Bess said.

"Why didn't you say he was wearing a red hat? That is a pretty clear descriptive item," said George.

"Be careful over there, George," I said.

George approached the man cautiously. She followed him for a bit, watching him carefully. She looked around to see if he was communicating with anyone else, if he had any accomplices. She didn't notice anyone else. Finally the man slowed down, and she walked up to him, and tapped him on the shoulder. As he turned around, we all noticed that he was holding a child in his arms. The child was holding a balloon and saying, "Follow the float, Daddy. Follow the float."

"Yes," the man said to George.

"I'm sorry," she said. "I thought you were someone else." George pulled back from the man and spoke into her cell phone. "False alarm. Bess and Nancy, this situation was a false alarm. He was holding a child."

"That's okay," I said. "Better that it's a false alarm than something worse."

"Sorry, Nancy," said Bess. "Like I said, I'm just very nervous and couldn't see the kid from here. I guess I'm a little on edge."

"Don't worry about it," I said. "We're all on edge. Honestly, it's better this way."

The spectators tossed more and more bouquets of flowers onto the deck of the float as it passed them. Lexi waved to the crowds, smiling and blowing kisses to them. I kept ducking as the flowers piled up all around me and flew past my head. Everything seemed to be going okay, and it looked like the parade was going to go on without any incident. I leaned back and relaxed more than I had all day and found myself waving and smiling at the crowds too. The parade was fun again, and I could tell from all the smiling faces in the crowd that it was an important part of the carnival festivities. I was glad to have listened to Mara.

Then the float jolted forward, lurching and shaking in tremors, like an earthquake. The engine growled, shaking the foundation of the float itself.

The float stopped moving as the band continued to march on, not knowing that the float had stalled and stopped dead in its tracks. Although stopped, the float continued to emit horrible growls and whines. Then there was a sound like a hiss as the shaking increased.

"Everything okay back there?" I asked Bess.

"Other than all the shaking and noise?" Bess asked. "I don't think this is so good."

"George, anything?" I asked.

"Nothing. Everything seems okay from here. The float is just not moving, and we can't hear the noises out here. I can hear them on the phone, but out here, it just looks like you guys stopped the float."

I stood and walked back to Lexi, who had a frightened look on her face even though she kept waving and blowing kisses as the flowers continued to pile up around her. I leaned over and whispered in her ear, "I am going to check on Officer Rees and make sure everything is okay with the engine."

"Please do," she said. "And hurry back."

I passed Bess and walked along the edge of the float to Officer Rees, who was struggling with the ignition. He looked up and saw me. He looked as pale and white with fear as Lexi.

"Nancy, I don't know what happened. It just got

jammed. The engine's still running, but the wheels aren't moving."

"Can you shut the engine off?" I asked.

"That's the weird thing. It won't shut off," he said. "You know how you can shut a car's engine off? This is supposed to work the same exact way, but it won't do that. Something's wrong here."

This was the moment I knew my prediction was about to come true. Between the noise and Officer Rees' description of the engine problems, it was only a matter of time before the float experienced greater issues.

"I'm going to grab Lexi and get off the float," I said. "We need to get off the float. You too. Get up and move." I turned to Bess and Lexi and yelled, "EVERYONE OFF THE FLOAT." But before I had a chance to reach them, George cried out over the phone.

"FIRE," she said. "FIRE. There's a fire on the float. Get off, Nancy. Bess, get off. Fire. Fire. Fire."

Bess shouted almost immediately afterward, "FIRE. FIRE."

Black smoke appeared as if out of nowhere, pouring out from underneath the float, billowing up into the air. I could hear the crowd calling out and acknowledging the fire, screaming and running in all directions. I made my way past Bess, who was still crouched down behind the throne. Blue and red flames appeared along the banister. The fresh coat of paint that was still wet caught fire fast. The flames spread quickly, circling the entire float, trapping us onboard. Lexi, Officer Rees, Bess, and I met in the middle of the float on the platform, keeping our distance from the heat and the flames.

"I knew this would happen. I knew something bad would happen. Oh, Nancy, do something. Help us, please," said Lexi.

"Nancy," Bess said, "we need to do something. We're trapped!"

I looked out over the crowd which was dispersing and scrambling in all directions, and made eye contact with George, who was still on the phone with me.

"George, go to the nearest food stand and grab a fire extinguisher," I said. "Every table should have one. Hurry. Please."

"Will do, Nancy," she said. "Sit tight." She quickly ran and got a fire extinguisher from the closest stand, then ran back to the float faster than ever. All the running she'd done from location to location today seemed to have prepared her for this very moment. She took a running start at the float before tossing the fire extinguisher over the banister like one of the bouquets of flowers. We all stepped back as it landed with a loud thud next to us. I picked it up, removed the pin, and squeezed the handle. White fire extinguisher foam doused the fire along the banister.

Nearby, I saw more white foam blasting the fire. As it settled and cleared, I could see that it was Ned and Dad helping to put out the flames.

"I'm here, Nancy," Ned called. "We're going to get you all off the float soon."

Ned and Dad continued to hose down the float from the street as I did from the deck of the float until the fire department arrived. Firefighters in full gear climbed aboard the float with their masks and hoses and axes and put out the remaining fire. They kicked out one of Bess's banisters and made a safe exit for us off the float and onto the ground, lifting us one by one down to the street.

All our parents had been watching from the crowd and ran to us, wrapping us up in hugs and many kisses. Dad was there too with Mrs. Gruen.

"Oh, Nancy," Dad said. "I was so scared. Are you okay?"

"Yes," I said. "I'm okay, but I knew this would happen. I tried to get Mara Stanfield to cancel the parade, but she wouldn't do it. Neither would the chief. No one wanted to listen to me. But I was right all along."

"Well, it's over now," he said.

Mrs. Gruen kissed me on the cheek and handed

me a bottle of water to drink to clear out the smoke from my throat. "Drink this, sweetie," she said. "It will help you to breathe."

"I demand that you stop working on this investigation immediately, Nancy," said Dad. "This has gotten far too dangerous for you to pursue. It is not child's play anymore. This is for the police to handle."

"But Dad—," I said, but he wouldn't listen to me at all.

"No. Stop. I care too much about your safety," he said. "You've obviously stumbled onto something dangerous. Someone doesn't like that you know as much as you do. Let's go find Chief McGinnis. You can tell him everything you know and then leave it all alone. Okay? Will you do that for me? Please?"

"Let's find Chief, Dad," I said. "He wanted to talk with you and me anyway. He thinks that I might have something to do with the stolen money."

"Seriously, Carson, this is out of hand," Mrs. Gruen said. "She's a teenager. This is all too much for a teenager to handle. Theft. Fire. No, no, no. Too much."

The float was doused in water by the fire department and the engine finally shut down. The decorations were burnt black and the flowers turned to ash. Lexi looked dazed as she gave her statement to the police, who had just arrived. They were interviewing everyone on the float as well as spectators who'd witnessed the fire erupt. Mara Stanfield came running over to us in tears, her purse still in her hands.

"Lexi, my goodness, I am so sorry. I had no idea," she said. "I'm so glad you are okay."

"Nancy warned you," said Lexi. "And you didn't listen. I'm wondering if you didn't have something to do with the fire yourself."

Chief McGinnis arrived on the scene and overheard this exchange. He whispered something into a policewoman's ear as she began to wrangle us all together—Bess, George, myself, Ned, Lexi, and Mara.

"I want to see all of you in the gymnasium right now. No questions. No answers. I have had it up to here," he said, raising his hand up to his head, "with all the lies and deception I've seen around here today. This was supposed to be a fun-filled day of celebration. It's the River Heights Celebration, after all. Now there are fires, stolen money, threats, mysterious notes. Well, no more. It ends right now."

"But sir," Mara said, but she was interrupted.

"No. Listen to me now. Everyone in the gym," he said. "We are going to get to the bottom of this. Because I think I know who is responsible." He looked at me and smiled.

"Her?" Mark Steele said, having just arrived. "Nancy Drew? Really, Chief."

Chief McGinnis didn't respond, which seemed to be a good enough answer for Mr. Steele, as he smiled too.

"Good thing you're an attorney, Carson," said Mr. Steele. "Looks like your little girl is going to need good representation, since Chief here thinks she's behind all the crimes today. The fire. The sabotage. And the stolen cash box money. Funny how she was conveniently around when all of these things happened."

I couldn't believe what I was hearing. I couldn't believe what they were all saying. Of course I wasn't behind the crimes. Why would I set fire to a float that I was on myself? Why would I steal money from my boyfriend, Ned? This was all so ludicrous. I had to find a way to prove my innocence.

PRADA PURSE EVIDENCE

"I am completely innocent," I said as I sat down on the bleachers next to George and Bess. Ned sat behind me with Lexi Claremont. Deirdre Shannon and her boyfriend, Josh, arrived too, keeping mostly to themselves at the end of the bleachers. Josh still looked a little green, either from all that food or fear of his parents finding out about his car accident. Mara Stanfield sat by herself in front of me, clutching her purse tight in her hands. She kept shaking her head in disbelief, at the fire on the float, at the torn dress, at being accused of stealing the ticket booth money. Mr. Nickerson, Mrs. Gruen, and my dad stood next to the bleachers, too nervous to sit down, as Mark Steele and Chief McGinnis paced in front of all of us. Mr. Steele had a perpetual frown on his face today. So many things had gone wrong that I was sure he was going to flip out on us.

"I really have nothing to do with any of this," I said again.

"Listen to her, Mark," Dad said. "You know Nancy. She's a good kid. You know deep down she had nothing to do with the fire. She didn't steal the money. She isn't writing the notes."

"Well, we're not so sure about that anymore," Mr. Steele said.

"How can you blame me for these crimes when I'm *investigating* them?" I queried. "I have information that links the criminal to all three—the fire, the missing money, and the threatening notes."

"A child investigating crime? Who ever heard of such a thing?" asked Mr. Steele, laughing. "Preposterous."

Dad, George, Ned, and Bess all looked at me, clearly nervous too.

"Enough," Chief McGinnis said. "This has gotten too far out of hand. Too dangerous. Too many people running around trying to help solve the mystery."

"But Chief," I said, "I didn't steal the money. I didn't start the fire. I didn't write any of those notes. You have to believe me."

He held up his hand and slowed me like a crossing guard holding up a sign. He nodded his head. "I know," he said. "Nancy Drew, you are not responsible for any of the crimes."

"What?" Mr. Steele said, confused. "But you said it was her. You said she was to blame."

"No," Chief said. "I said I knew who was responsible, and I looked at Nancy, but I never said her name. Do not jump to conclusions, please."

I was not entirely sure why Mark Steele seemed to want to see me get in trouble for all of this. Maybe he just wanted it all to be solved and made to disappear, whether I was the real culprit or not.

"Nancy Drew did not commit any of these crimes," Chief McGinnis said.

"Thank goodness," Mrs. Gruen chimed in from the back of the room, fanning herself with her hand.

"But I do want to hear what evidence you were able to uncover," Chief continued. "I have some information myself, and I think before I reveal what I know, I would like to hear what you know." He stepped back and welcomed me up to stand next to him and present my information to the group.

"Well," I said, "I had a few suspects early on, each with peculiar circumstances, but none with a real motive. I examined Deirdre and Josh for a bit and thought they were some kind of team, working together to steal the money and plant the notes."

"Hey," Deirdre said angrily. "How dare you, Nancy Drew!"

"But I needed to ask myself, what would they have to gain?" I said. "And the answer is nothing. They would gain nothing at all. It was not them."

Deirdre and Josh smiled at me.

"Thanks," said Deirdre.

"Then I thought maybe it was Joshua Andrews, the baker," I said. "Mr. Steele here refused to rent him a food stand, so the motive existed. Mr. Andrews was angry that he couldn't participate in the carnival, so perhaps he decided to sabotage it. With fire. With notes. By stealing the money. But the only problem was that it would have been impossible for him to have done all those things and been at his bakery in town."

"That's right," Mrs. Gruen said. "I saw him this morning."

"Exactly," I said. "Mrs. Gruen saw Mr. Andrews at his bakery at the same time that Ned claims the ticket booth money was stolen. Mr. Nickerson saw him at the bakery too."

"What about Ned Nickerson, then?" said Mr. Steele.

"That is just ridiculous," Ned said, sitting forward in his seat. "We already went through this. I didn't steal anything."

"Not my boy," Mr. Nickerson said.

"Correct. Also, impossible," I said. "First of all, where would Ned have hidden the money if he had stolen it, and more important, when would he have had the time to hide it? Between opening the ticket booth and assisting all his unexpected callers and visitors, when would he have found time to leave the ticket booth and hide the money away? Besides, Josh, Deirdre, and Mara each claim to have stopped by and had an interaction with Ned. This proves that he never left."

"All right, Nancy," Chief McGinnis said. "Thank you for the recap, but what is the evidence that you discovered?"

"I discovered smudges on the notes," I said, "that looked different from the ink the notes were written in, so I asked George to use her new scientific machine to examine the elemental makeup of the smudges."

"What was the smudge?" Chief McGinnis asked.

"Ballaster Ink," I said.

"Is that supposed to mean something?" asked Mr. Steele.

Mr. Nickerson cleared his throat and raised his hand like he was in a classroom, waiting to be called on by the teacher.

"Yes," Chief said, pointing at him.

"Allow me to explain Ballaster Ink," he said. "As publisher of the *River Heights Bugle*, I am constantly looking for ways to compete with the bigger national daily newspapers. One of the ways in which I am able to do this is by using a less expensive ink for my newspaper. Ballaster Ink. There are many daily, weekly, and monthly newspapers that use this ink in their pages. The only downside is that it comes off on your fingers more easily than regular ink."

"I'm sorry, but I don't think I follow," Chief McGinnis said.

"Whoever is writing the notes, whoever ripped up Lexi's dress, they read a lot of these smaller newspapers," I said. "The ink comes off easier onto your fingers. No matter how much you wash your hands, the ink is difficult to get off. Which is why we found the smudges on the notes and on the dress."

"So you were able to tie the notes and the dress together, but how are we supposed to tie those to the money and the fire?" Mark Steele said.

"The notes threatened future sabotage, ever since yesterday, in fact. The notes even mentioned the parade," I said. "So the fact that the notes specifically warned us that more sabotage would take place, and then it did, only proves the connection."

"Interesting," Chief McGinnis said.

"And finally," I said, "one of you here is responsible for this annoying nickname."

"What's wrong with Fancy Nancy?" Mark Steele asked.

Even Mr. Steele knew about it. I couldn't have been more frustrated.

"One of you is responsible for telling people to call me this name. And I want to know who it is."

"Thank you, Fancy Nancy, for the evidence." Chief smirked. "However, I have already decided who the criminal is, and it saddens me to have to tell you."

"Who is it?" I asked.

We all looked at one another, passing glances and worried expressions. Any one of us could have been accused of these crimes. Chief paced back and forth in front of the bleachers, finally stopping in front of Mara Stanfield.

"Mara?" asked Mr. Steele. "No."

"It wasn't me," she said. "No, I didn't do it."

"Yes," Chief said. "I am sorry to say, but Mara Stanfield is the thief, the author of the notes, and the arsonist."

Mark Steele marched over to Mara, shaking his head in disgust. He put his hands on his hips and stared at her. I could tell he wanted to believe her, to believe that she didn't do it, but he seemed to be exhausted with all the trouble and ready to accept the chief's findings.

"Mara," Mr. Steele said, "I suggest that you resign as president of the board of the Daughters of River Heights association."

"Mark," she said. "I'm telling the truth here. I didn't do any of these things."

"I'm sorry," he said. "I should have listened to my gut instinct. I always had a feeling you were involved. Let me ask you this one question: Why didn't you listen to Nancy when she asked you to stop the parade?"

"Why didn't *you* listen to Nancy?" she asked. "She's been running around this carnival all day, asking questions and poking her nose where it doesn't belong, but you never listened to her either."

"I believe I just finished listening to her," he said. "Why don't you just resign gracefully? This will avoid any negative press."

"This is absurd," she said. "You have no proof of any of this. I am calling an emergency board meeting. I have no obligation to resign, especially without any evidence. I am utterly shocked and insulted at these horrible accusations." Mara dug through her purse for her phone, but had difficulty finding it and continued to root and root for it. "I mean, setting fire to our float? With students aboard? Are you serious?

What kind of person do you take me for anyway?"

"A guilty person," Mr. Steele said.

"Mara," said Chief, "you are the only one connected to all aspects of these incidents. You were seen at the ticket booth this morning. You are the president of the Daughters of River Heights Association and the head of the parade committee. You were there when the dress was destroyed. And you've been seen around the food court area, in the vicinity of the notes."

"So have a lot of us," she said, her hand sliding in and out of purse pockets, still looking for her cell phone. "What would my motive be?"

"You wanted to head up the carnival committee and oversee everything, but Mark Steele stood in your way," Chief said. "If you sabotaged his carnival in every way possible, then you would be put in charge next year in place of Mark. If you were lucky, you would be instated this year, replacing Mark immediately."

"This is absolutely insane," she said, standing to leave. "I will not sit here and listen to this any longer. Why can't I find my phone?" Just then her purse fell to the floor. The contents spilled out across the gymnasium floor—a bundle of cash wrapped in a blue note.

The room was uncomfortably quiet as we all stared

at the cash. Chief McGinnis pulled a rubber band off the wad and unfolded the blue note. Black smudges were smeared all over the paper. Chief counted out the cash and looked up when he finished. He handed the cash over to Mark Steele.

"Mark, I believe this is exactly the amount that was stolen—three hundred and fifty dollars," Chief said.

"My, oh, my," said Mr. Steele. "Why, it is the missing money. Thank you, Chief." He smiled at the chief, then at me. "Sorry for the accusation, Nancy."

"I don't understand this," Mara said, still rifling through her purse. "Why can't I find any of my belongings in here? Where is my cell phone? Where is my wallet? Where are my car keys?"

"Mara Stanfield," Chief said, "you are under arrest for petty larceny, arson, and terrorizing River Heights with threats."

"Chief, you have to believe me. I don't know where that money came from. It wasn't me. I swear to you, it wasn't me," she said, pleading.

"The evidence doesn't lie," Chief McGinnis said, pulling out handcuffs and slapping them onto her wrists behind her back, exposing her fingers.

"Wait," I yelled from the bleachers. "Look at her fingers."

"Why would we do that?" Chief said.

"They're clean. She doesn't have any black ink on them," I said. "The person we're looking for will have hands stained with black ink."

"Honestly," Mark Steele said. "Chief, are you seriously going to take investigative advice from Nancy Drew? She probably washed them really well not too long ago."

"Watch it, Mark," said Chief.

Suddenly Bess shrieked. Everyone jumped from shock and turned to look at her as she threw herself to the ground, rifling through Mara Stanfield's purse.

"It's a fake," said Bess. "It's a fake. It's a fake."

"What do you mean?" George asked.

"And there are smudges inside the purse," Bess said.

"Can someone please explain to me what is going on?" said Chief.

"Earlier today I saw that Mara was carrying a very expensive purse. A Prada purse," Bess said. "Do you know how high-end the brand Prada is, Chief?"

"I am vaguely aware of the name," he said. "It is very expensive. Continue."

"Well, then you also know how it is spelled. And this is definitely not a Prada purse," said Bess.

"How do you know?" Mr. Steele asked.

Bess held up the purse to show everyone the

inside—Pradi. Black smudges were visible along the lining too.

"How is it that her purse has black smudges all over it, but her fingers don't? How is it that she couldn't find her cell phone, or wallet, but the ticket booth money was tied up neatly in a stack, covered by a blue note?" I said. "Someone is trying to frame Mara for this."

"Impossible," Mr. Steele said.

"I believe the evidence is pointing you in a different direction, Chief," said Dad.

"Who was your source of information who said Mara was responsible for all of this?" George asked.

"I received an anonymous phone call. Whoever it was said that Mara Stanfield was to blame for the crimes today and that proof could be found in her purse," said Chief. "It does seem a little too tidy."

"Don't you think that I would have hidden the money away somewhere if I had stolen it, so that it wasn't in my purse all day?" Mara asked. "And why would I have paid for float alterations, if I was just going to torch it?"

"Chief," I said. "I don't mean any disrespect here, but I believe that you've arrested the wrong person. Mara is innocent."

Chief looked at me and the rest of us, before grabbing the handcuffs still snapped onto Mara's wrists and walking her out of the gymnasium and into the back of his squad car. We followed them outside and watched as Mara began to cry. She looked at me through the window and mouthed the words, *Please help me.*

"Nancy," George said. "We have to do something."

"I know," I said.

"But what?" Bess asked. "Chief has made up his mind. They found the cash in Mara's possession."

"We need to find more evidence," I said. "There has to be something. There's no way that Mara is responsible for any of it."

"Not even your new name?" Bess said.

"Not even the name that drives me crazy," I said.

BRAND-NEW DAY

None of the evidence pointed to Mara. Sure, the ticket booth money was found in her purse. Yes, she had motive. Absolutely, she had access to all the crime scenes—the ticket booth, the food court, Lexi's dress, and the parade float. And because of all those things and the fact that Chief McGinnis found the bundle of cash wrapped in a blue note in her purse, she'd been arrested and was sitting in the back of a police car.

Aly Stanfield, Mara's daughter, stood next to the police car, her hand on the window. Mara's hand was up too, pressed against the glass. Aly cried, never moving her hand.

"Mom," she said. "What can I do to get you out of here?"

"It's okay, baby," Mara said. "This is just a misunderstanding."

"But what can I do? There has to be something I can do to get you out of here. Chief McGinnis is wrong."

"He is wrong, baby. But it will all be okay."

I overheard their conversation and eased my way between them.

"Mara. Aly. I just might have an idea," I said.

"What's that?" Aly asked, removing her hand from the glass of the window.

"Bess and I know that the purse wasn't yours. We saw yours earlier today—the Prada purse. This one clearly said Pradi on it, but Chief wouldn't know the difference in a million years."

"So what are you suggesting?" Mara asked.

"That we find the other purse. That we find *your* purse. It has to be around here somewhere."

"What a good idea," Aly said.

"I just don't know where it could be," said Mara.

"Well, when was the last time you saw your purse? Or when was the last time that you left your purse unattended? My thought is that whoever is doing all this sabotage tried to frame you. The perpetrator loaded you up with evidence and hung you out to dry. However, the criminal still had to have handled your real purse. It has to be somewhere."

Mara thought for a minute. Then said, "The fro-yo stand."

"That's right," said Aly. "You stopped by to give me money for the rides and left your purse behind the table with the girls."

"Could it have been Deirdre?" I asked. Suddenly Deirdre's name had popped up again. She had access to the purse and the ticket booth money and the blue notes, but the idea of Deirdre Shannon taking on the role of supervillain just didn't feel right.

"No," Aly said. "Deidre disappeared around the time that you showed up at the fro-yo stand this morning. I've seen her around the carnival, but she never came back to help out."

"What did you do with the money I gave you this morning?" Mara asked. "You said you needed it for rides, but I don't think I saw you get on any."

"Don't be mad," said Aly. "You always get mad about this."

"Aly, what did you do?" Mara asked.

"I went to see Lucia Gonsalvo."

Mara dropped her head forward, frustrated. She looked at me and glared, like she was mad that I'd let Aly go to Ms. Gonsalvo. For all intents and purposes, Lucia Gonsalvo was the local psychic and owner of the Psychic's Parlor in town. She looked exotic, as one would imagine a psychic to look, but she had also lived in River Heights ever since I could remember. Dad had actually represented her once in a legal case with her landlord. He'd been able to sort out her issue amicably without having to take it to court. I wondered if she psychically saw that Carson Drew could help her resolve her problems and that was why she used him.

Lucia Gonsalvo had a tiny tent at the carnival, and often there were small lines of people waiting outside, anxious to meet with her. Most of the time, her clients at the carnival were out-of-towners or visitors. But occasionally, a few locals would seek her advice. Aly Stanfield, apparently, being one of them.

"What did she say?" Mara asked, adjusting her handcuffed hands in her lap and resting her head against the seat. "Did she foresee that your mother would be arrested by the end of the day?"

"She said that I had important things to do today."

"Like bail your mommy out of jail," Mara said.

"And she said that I would be back to see her before the sun went down."

"Listen," I said. "I'm going back to the fro-yo stand with Aly to look for your real purse. When the switch took place, I have a feeling that whoever did it had to ditch your real purse right away. So it has to be around there somewhere. In a garbage can or under a table somewhere."

"Please hurry," Mara said. "I can't stand to be here any longer than I have to be. Besides, as soon as Chief McGinnis comes back, he's going to take me in to the police station."

I turned to Bess and George and explained the game plan.

"The four of us can cover more ground than just Aly and me. We're looking for the real Prada purse," I said. "We have to look everywhere."

Bess frowned. "Oh, poor Prada purse."

"What's wrong now?" asked George.

"It hurts me to think about that poor baby purse being in a dark place somewhere," she said. "Or buried under gross garbage. We need to find her."

"Let's just hope that all her personal belongings are still inside. Her car keys. Her wallet. Her cell phone. These will help us to prove beyond a doubt that Mara was framed."

We headed off together, back into the carnival on a very important specific mission. I felt closer than ever to finding answers, and I believed everything hinged on the real Prada purse.

Back at the fro-yo stand, the four of us ransacked every inch of space. Under the table. Under napkins.

On top of the fro-yo machine. Inside the fro-yo machine. In the garbage can. Nothing. We didn't find the purse—or a single shred of evidence that proved her purse had ever been left there.

Aly and Bess moved outside the stand and checked behind other tables. The candy apple table. The popcorn table. The funnel cake table. Nothing.

George and I left the food court and wandered around the games and rides section of the carnival, checking more trash cans, but we also asked the operators and cash collectors if they had seen anything suspicious, or if they had witnessed anyone hiding or dumping a purse somewhere. No one remembered seeing or hearing anything. Although they had all heard about the drama of the day—missing money, blue notes, dress devastation, and parade float sabotage.

Finally George and I met up with Aly and Bess. We had swept through the entire carnival, searching high and low, left and right for the purse.

"The purse is our only hope," Aly said, "to prove my mom's innocence."

"There has to be another way," said George.

"George is right," Bess said. "This can't be the end of the road. We've chased this mystery all day. We've been all over the place, investigated so many people. It just can't end here. It can't end on a missing purse."

"Wait a minute," I said. "Just hold on. I think I have an idea." It was then that the greatest and most unorthodox idea popped into my head. "You guys are going to think I'm a little crazy, and I would never use this method under any other circumstances, but since we've run out of options, what if we go and see Lucia Gonsalvo?"

"Nancy, are you sure you want to do that?" asked Bess.

"It seems like a long shot, but what do we really have to lose at this point?" George said.

"And she did tell me earlier today that I would be back to see her soon," Aly said.

"You never know what information she'll have for us," I said. "Worst-case scenario is that she tells us absolutely nothing. Best-case scenario is that she gives us a nudge in the right direction."

The girls looked at one another and thought a minute before agreeing to join the plan. Bess and George smiled, giddy, I thought, about visiting a psychic—something they had never done before.

"Well," I said. "Is everybody onboard with the idea?"

"Let's go," said George.

"Why not," Bess said.

We walked through the rides and food court sections to a tiny tent on the outskirts of the carnival.

Lucia Gonsalvo sat in a rocking chair outside, sipping iced tea. She wore a long brown skirt and a red shoulder wrap, and her hair was wrapped up in a bandanna. As we approached, she stopped rocking and closed her eyes. She turned her face up toward the sky and let the sun's rays beat down on her as she soaked up the warmth. She inhaled a big breath and exhaled slowly. "Welcome," she said, her eyes still closed.

"I came back," Aly said. "Just like you predicted."

"Yes you did, my child," she said.

"We were wondering if you would be able to help us," I said. "We're trying to solve a mystery and find a purse, but we've run out of conventional means to help us. I thought maybe if we came to you, you would be able to help us in some way."

Ms. Gonsalvo began rocking in her chair again as a black cat ran out from inside the tent and hopped into her lap. She pet the cat from its head down to the tip of its tail, over and over. "You want my help, huh?"

"Yes," I said. "Very much so."

"Please," she said, "follow me." Ms. Gonsalvo stood, still holding the cat, and walked into her tent. All four of us entered behind her, unsure if what we were doing was brilliant or crazy.

Inside, there was a table with a crystal ball in the

center of it and five chairs. We sat down around the table and stared at the crystal ball intensely, like we expected a dragon or monster to climb out of it. Ms. Gonsalvo put the cat back down on the floor and placed her hands on the crystal ball, closing her eyes. She tilted her head back and began chanting nonsensical words.

I knew that I was as nervous as the other girls, having never done something like this before. We all held hands, waiting for Ms. Gonsalvo to give us some insight or information about our case.

"You are looking for a purse," she said. "But it is missing and you can't find it. Someone has hidden it from you and you are desperate to find it."

"Go on," I said.

"And you have many unanswered questions."

"We do," I said. "Can you help us answer some of them?"

"The person you are looking for cannot be found today," she said. "The person has covered his or her tracks too well. Not even I can see who it is."

"Can you tell if it's a man or a woman?" Bess asked.

"I cannot," she said. "But I can tell you that the purse is where it all began. Go back to the beginning and you will find it."

"The beginning?" asked Aly. "What does that mean?"

"The beginning of what?" George asked.

"Guys," I said, nearly jumping out of my seat. "The beginning of this case. Where did it begin?" The girls didn't catch on. "The ticket booth. It began with the missing ticket booth money."

"Oh my gosh," Aly said. "We were just there."

"The purse is there," Ms. Gonsalvo said. "Go and you will find it."

"Is that all you see?" I asked.

"That is all," she said.

I slid ten dollars across the table to her, and we stood to leave the tent. As we reached the opening, she called out to us.

"Wait," she said. "He is close."

"Who is close?" I said.

"The person you are looking for," she said. "He is close."

"It's a guy. We're looking for a guy?" I asked.

"But I can't make out his face. He has ink on his fingers. He stole the money. He stole the purse. He wrote the notes. He sabotaged the float."

"Who is it?" Bess blurted out.

"I can't see him," she said. "But it's not that I can see him, there is something telling me about this."

"What are you talking about?" I asked.

"There is video footage. A security camera," she

said. "In the school. Check the security camera and you will find him."

We were about to leave again when Ms. Gonsalvo spoke once more. "Wait. There is one more thing." She looked at me and pointed. "Fancy Nancy," she said. "You don't like it when people call you by that name."

"No," I said. "I hate that name. How did you know about that?"

"Speak with Heather. She knows about it," Ms. Gonsalvo said.

"Heather Harris?" I asked. I looked at Aly to see if she knew anything about this, but she avoided eye contact. "Aly? Do you know something that you're not telling me?" I looked at George and Bess, who looked away as well. "Girls? Someone needs to fess up here."

"Heather was mad that you busted her and her blog yesterday, and she wanted to get back at you, so she made fun of the way you dressed at the fro-yo stand. She called you Fancy Nancy," Aly said. "I heard it from her."

"I heard it from Aly," Bess said.

"I heard it from Bess," said George.

"And who told my dad?" I asked.

"I did," Bess said. "I asked if Fancy Nancy was there, and he laughed."

I had bigger things to worry about than that silly name, but I was happy to have gotten to the bottom of that mystery. I thanked Lucia Gonsalvo again as the four of us rushed out of her tent and back to the ticket booth. Mr. Nickerson and Dad were there with Ned. Mr. Steele was speaking with Chief McGinnis.

"I have an important announcement to make," I said, "and I need everyone to listen."

"Everyone is listening, dear," Dad said.

"Chief, if my source is correct, then Mara's real purse with all her belongings was stolen and replaced by the fake purse. Her real purse was stashed inside the ticket booth."

"Well, then, let's open it back up and see for ourselves," Chief said.

Ned and Mr. Steele walked over to the door of the ticket booth and unlocked it. They both went inside with Chief McGinnis and emerged again almost right away, the chief holding Mara's real—and according to Bess, very expensive—Prada purse. Chief opened the purse and pulled out a wallet and a cell phone. He opened the wallet and removed Mara's driver's license.

"Looks like we have conflicting evidence," said Chief. "Here's her real purse, but Nancy, that still doesn't prove she didn't take the money in the first place. She could have easily stashed her purse in the ticket booth herself."

"There is one more piece of evidence," I said, turning to face Mr. Steele. "Are there surveillance cameras attached to the school?"

"Yes, there are, but none that would have picked up any of the carnival activity," he said.

"But what about the parking lot? What about the ticket booth?" I asked. "Are there any cameras that would have captured even a little bit of footage?"

He thought for a moment before answering. "Actually, you know, yes. There just might be one camera that picked something up."

"Well, then, let's review that tape," Chief McGinnis said.

In the front office of the school, Chief McGinnis, Mark Steele, Bess, Ned, Mr. Nickerson, Aly Stanfield, and I stood around a television as George operated the video machine. We watched as the sun came up at the beginning of the day and a few cars began to arrive and park in the lot.

"There I am," Mr. Steele said, pointing to his car parking under a grove of trees.

George fast-forwarded a bit. Then Mr. Steele began to yell for her to stop.

"Wait. Rewind," he said. "Go back."

George backed up a bit before stopping again. "Here?"

"Yes," he said. "Watch." He pointed at his car again, parked and still. Nothing happened for a few minutes, but then another car came into the picture. I knew right away what was about to happen. It was Josh, Deirdre's boyfriend. He was backing his parents' car into the spot when—*BAM!*—*CRASH!*—he tore up the side of Mark Steele's car. Josh ran around both cars, examining the damage. He then ran across the parking lot to the ticket booth, which was in the corner of the camera. He returned minutes later with paper and a pen and left a note on the windshield.

"He hit my car," Mr. Steele said. "That was my car! How come no one told me that he hit my car?" He paced in the back of the room, holding his head.

We continued to look at the footage and saw Deirdre and Mara both knock on the ticket booth door and speak to someone inside—Ned. They were very far away and difficult to see, but because we had a time line in place already, we knew who we were looking at. It was then that something interesting happened. A fourth person arrived at the ticket booth door, but this person didn't stand outside like the others. This person entered and exited soon after with the cash box in their hands.

"Did you all see that?" I said.

"We did," said Chief.

"I can't make out who it is," Ned said. "It's too blurry and too far away."

"But it is definitely a man," Chief said.

Mr. Steele turned to Ned. "You told us only three people stopped at the ticket booth this morning. You failed to mention a fourth."

"Ned, can you please explain?" said Chief.

Ned tuned pale and looked at me.

"Ned made me promise not to say anything, but after Mara stopped by the stand this morning," I said, "he fell asleep."

"You what?" Mr. Steele yelled.

"It was early. I was tired. I'm sorry. It's my fault the money was stolen, but I didn't steal it. That dude right there did," Ned said.

George fast-forwarded a while before stumbling on the last piece of the puzzle. "Um, hey, everyone. Look."

Outside the ticket booth and closer to the camera stood Ned, his dad, and me. We were talking. This was only a few hours ago, and I remembered it well. Behind us, however, was the mysterious man again, carrying a woman's purse. He snuck back into the ticket booth with the purse and left without it.

"Holy cow," Ned said. "Did you all see that?"

"It appears that I have arrested the wrong individual," said Chief.

"Arrest Ned Nickerson," Mr. Steele said.

"No, Mark," Chief said. "He didn't do anything wrong. Sleeping is not a crime. It's negligent, but not a crime."

"So what does this mean?" Bess asked.

"It means Mara is innocent. Ned is innocent. Deirdre and Josh are innocent. It means that we still have no idea who stole the money, framed Mara, sabotaged the float, or wrote the notes. But we do know it is a man."

Everyone was quiet. One by one, we left the front office and headed back to the parking lot, each to our own car, to head home after another long day. I stayed behind and continued to rewind the video footage. Back to the beginning where the thief snuck into the ticket booth and left holding the cash box. I froze the screen and stared at the image.

"Who in the world are you?" I asked. "And why are you doing this?" These questions remained unanswered for now, but I was sure the mystery would soon be solved. "I will find you," I said. "Just give it time." I turned off the television and video equipment and headed home. Tomorrow would be a brand-new day.